ILER FO

Qty _____ Date _____

Qty _____ Date _____

Cut By: _____

Scanned By: _____

Scanned B

"What do you get when you mash up literary stars with exciting new voices? You get *African Roar 2011*. A fantastic collection of short stories with diverse voices covering a range of narratives and styles... Confident, imaginative, electrifying, *African Roar 2011* is a treat for lovers of the short story everywhere."— Tendai Huchu, author of *The Hairdresser of Harare*.

"*African Roar 2011* is a compelling collection of short stories with some of the big and emerging names in contemporary African writing. This cocktail of a book touches on diverse themes and sensibilities, weaving an intricate tapestry of modern tales."— Jude Dibia, author of *Blackbird* and *Unbridled*, and a recipient of the Ken Saro-Wiwa Prose Prize and Commonwealth Writers Highly Commended Award.

"At a time when the short story is regaining popularity, this anthology showcases the form at its vibrant best. *African Roar 2011* is a striking and exciting collection of stories. Read and revel in them."— Jayne Bauling, South African novelist and poet, and winner of the 2009 Macmillan Writer's Prize for Africa and the 2011 Maskew Miller Longman literature award.

"*African Roar 2011* is a well-prepared dish that offers a rich blend of literary delicacies; from the practised ink of the chefs, to the talented pens of the emerging writers, flow the rich creative ingredients that stew these pages into a most enjoyable story collection. The stories reflect the diversity of the tree from which they are plucked; the rich literary talent that has its roots in

Africa. An exciting read."— Novuyo Rosa Tshuma, short fiction writer and recipient of the 2009 Yvonne Vera Award.

"Encompassing a wide variety of diverse voices, *African Roar 2011* showcases a smorgasbord of new and established writers. Fiction and memoir sit comfortably side by side in this intriguing collection, which puts paid once and for all to the myth of a monolithic African culture."— Fiona Snyckers, author of the *Trinity* series of novels, and the *Sisterz* series of mobile novels.

"The fourteen short stories in *African Roar 2011* are fourteen voices in a wide and beautiful range. They're parables or fables, classically realistic, or savagely satiric, morality tales, haunting tales, or tales with intoxicating oral cadences. There are brilliant imaginings of other consciousnesses. They're stories that take you deep into the hearts and minds of characters, and to places new yet familiar, and places quite strange. This anthology showcases dynamic voices coming from all over Africa and the African Diaspora right now, and they're exhilarating indeed."— Dawn Promislow, author of the collection *Jewels and Other Stories.*

"A salmagundi of wordsmiths that offers an array of narratives located in gritty African Realism interspersed with moments of magical realism and laugh-out-loud humour. A fitting tribute to the late Ruzvidzo Stanley Mupfudza, this anthology is a multifaceted authentic voice of Africa. A truly visceral reading experience as the stories unfolded from the pages and wrapped their filmic imagery around my mind."— Gillian Schutte, award winning documentary filmmaker, writer, and social justice activist. Author of two collections of poetry and debut novel *'After just now'*, founder of the human rights forum Media for Justice, and the independent Ludic Press.

"*African Roar 2011* will leave its reader with longing, sadness and optimism. Each story in this year's collection captures the spirit of our lives right now: struggle and pain are still alive, yet there's a sense of something exciting, some big change that's to come. From the opening story by Ruzvidzo Stanley Mupfudza (to whom this anthology is dedicated) about two outcasts whose fates get overturned to a writer-turned-crook, husbands struggling to be faithful, media and political scandals, the horrifying downfall of a well-to-do family, and many more, we see life on the African continent from its tiniest citizens to those in 'high places'. Death and real horror hover over a lot of the stories, yet humour and hope are never far off. The stories are raw, sharp, suspenseful, and full of momentum and liveliness. I was turning pages, finding threads between characters — regardless of where their stories took root — and I could not stop thinking about these riveting stories for days." — Ayesha Harruna Attah, author of *Harmattan Rain*, short-listed for the 2010 Commonwealth Writers' Prize.

African Roar 2011

Edited by
Emmanuel Sigauke
& Ivor Hartmann

A StoryTime Publication

African Roar 2011 Copyright © 2011 StoryTime

Each contribution remains under the © copyright of the author

Cover Image © 'Marange' by Victor Mavedzenge
(http://www.mavedzenge.com/)
Used by permission

ISBN: 978-0-9870089-4-7

This anthology is dedicated to

Ruzvidzo Stanley Mupfudza

(8th January 1971 - 3rd May 2010)

Contents

Ruzvidzo Stanley Mupfudza

(A tribute by Memory Chirere)

Ruzvidzo. You cannot go just like that. I only learnt about it a day after, when I phoned the guys at BWAZ [Budding Writers Association of Zimbabwe] over an otherwise happy matter. I didn't know you had been ill in hospital. For over six months you were unreachable. You had suddenly disappeared from the social scene. This was not the first time that you disappeared from the scene.

You took a very quick and solitary exit.

A week before your death, I bumped into Ignatius Mabasa at an Avondale ice cream shop and he said he had seen you! He said you had talked. And as the kids ran around, licking their ice creams and bantering amongst themselves, Ignatius said you said you felt that most of what you had written in the past was rather bleak and you were reworking some of your unpublished stories and poems (and novels too) because you now realised that, after all, life was a positive thing. We were impressed and were almost certain that one full volume of your work would eventually come out.

And now-this!

Is this the end of the end? Always the more courageous, I hope you faced your end with courage.

We first met in 1991 at the University of Zimbabwe. We went to English, History, and Economic History, classes together. One afternoon you came to my room NCI F105. Being a day scholar, you wanted somewhere quiet to sit and do some work. I went down to the foyer to pick the 4 pm tea (to think they served free teas then!). When I came back with two cups (yours and mine), you said you didn't take tea!

We were strangers then. As I slowly went through the two cups, you said you had heard from people that I sometimes scribbled some poems and stories. You also wondered why I was reluctant to be referred to as a writer. I am not published yet, I said. You laughed loud and long and I thought you were a proud little fellow.

A writer does not need to publish to be called a writer, you argued. A writer writes, you added. Later, I got to see your point.

Then I asked about your totem and your roots and you argued that totems tended to take us backward. Totems were old things. You said that you were a cosmopolitan man, something like that. I quietly sympathised with you! This is in contrast to recent times when you became a fierce Pan-Africanist and an avid follower of African traditions.

It is about this time that you began to say you wanted to be free. You said it regularly and pompously too and it began to overflow into your seminar presentations in class. We laughed at it: Dudziro Nhengu, Nhamu Tamari, Khumbulani Phiri, and I. Can anyone in this world be free, we wondered. You even talked about being a 'free spirit' and that became your nickname.

You quarrelled bitterly with those who taught us 'Literature and Socialism' and 'Theories of Literature', and we asked you to be careful because that was a sure way of failing. But, strangely, they let you off the hook for things all of us could have been punished for. To demonstrate your desire for freedom, you started attending a certain meditative oriental art form somewhere on Pendennis Road. You said your lady instructor taught you self-defence and soul searching. You said you were being taught to see the world 'from inside one's soul'. You developed a distant look in your eyes that never left you. The way a bird looks into space after taking a sip of water from the trough.

Then a few months later you suddenly changed and joined the Shorin Ryu Karate club on campus.

We began to take writing more seriously. We joined the writing class conducted by Chenjerai Hove — the writer-

in-residence then. There were many of us in there: Nhamo
Mhiripiri, Ignatius Mabasa, Joyce Mutiti, Emmanuel
Sigauke, Zvisinei Sandi, Thabisani Ndlovu, Eresina
Hwede, and others. Our mentor had just won the NOMA
Award but behaved like he had just simply sold a goat.
Hove listened as we read out our stories. Then he would
close his eyes, hold his chest and say: 'Vapfanha, writing
comes from here'. We laughed at that but up until your
death; we slowly awakened to the message behind that
riddle. You will remember my story in which a writer's
book causes a revolution! I had set the story in South
America. Why did I hope to succeed with a story set in
unfamiliar lands? Naivety.

Then there was the trip that the three of us, Ignatius
Mabasa, you and I, made to Bulawayo on the invitation of
author Chiedza Musengezi. She was working on a script for
a children's book and she wanted us 'to tear it apart'. What
a weekend! It was our first time in Bulawayo.

For a couple of days we chatted deep into the night,
reading out loud and critiquing one another's works. Then
on a Sunday morning Chiedza asked us to 'just go out and
see Bulawayo for yourselves.' That was good. But, as soon
as we got to a bar in a semi industrial area near Malindela,
you and I (because Ignatius does not drink), had one, two,
and maybe three each, and Ignatius reminded us that we
needed to move on.

You refused flatly. You said you wanted to see the soul of
Bulawayo because there was much of it in this bar and we
should hang around longer. We quarrelled bitterly and this
is the closest that you and I ever came to blows.

We dragged you out as you held an unfinished pint. I said
nasty things about you and you retaliated. Finally Ignatius
intervened, when in fact he had caused the altercation
himself by suggesting we move on. He and I went out to
explore Bulawayo and you stubbornly walked back into the
bar. Later, you said you had walked out too and explored
Bulawayo all by yourself. We met again in the evening at

Chiedza's place. Strangely, we were all cheerful and I think to this day, Chiedza has not learnt about this.

After UZ, I went to teach at Chipindura High in Bindura and you went to Oriel Boys High. During one of my visits, I noticed that your students 'worshipped' you. Their teacher was a celebrity. You had written a very powerful article in the *Moto* magazine about the sticking point of race relations in Zimbabwe. There was uproar in academic circles. You were in the papers and on TV. Judith Todd herself paid you a visit at home to congratulate you.

You allowed your pupils some liberties which other teachers did not. You asked them to think freely. No wonder that some of your former students like Mabasa Sasa later became your workmates. I began to look forward to a novel because I think you had many such scripts.

You were a self-confessed admirer of Dambudzo Marechera. In an article in *The Herald* of 2nd May 2001, page 7, you admit that you had 'once walked in the shadow of Marechera' before finally finding your own voice. You proceed: "Now, I am grown, I have not stopped questing for and exploring new horizons... the roads and the journeys I take are mine and not Marechera's. Whereas he would balk at the thought of being levelled 'an African writer', I have become a fierce Pan-Africanist."

From Marechera, you adopted a hypnotic and intense writing style. But as evident in your stories like 'The Eyes of a Walk' and 'Mermaid Out of the Rain', you adopted a fusion of Marechera with the charmed realism of Allende and Marquez. There is a suggestion that you felt that while Marechera was brilliant, he needed to dig deeper and benefit more from African folk, myth, and wisdom.

I think your days at Ibbo Mandaza's Mirror Group of papers will always stand out. You were the Acting Editor of the *Sunday Mirror* for a long time. You wrote lengthy articles under the title 'Muhera Wekwa Pfumojena'.You wrote about the return to Guruuswa, the return to Gomba rekwaNyashanu. This was no simple mythical quest.

11

You wanted to say, I think, that we need to return to the source. Not to go back to matehwe and nhembe, but to go back and reconnect with our upward thrust in history. To go back and pick again those values and qualities which are enduring and timeless, in order to face the present.

For me this was the most dramatic stretch in your life. The *Sunday Mirror* was something to look forward to. With a crop of writers like Mabasa Sasa, Laura Chiweshe, Phillip Chidavaenzi, Trust Khosa, and others, you were destined for great heights. Yes, there was also the Scrutator! You gave more space to the Arts and features in a way that has no comparison to this day in Zimbabwe.

I remember that you bought various sets of mbiras and placed them along your guitar in your study and learnt to play both at the same time. You started to draw too, having felt that maybe the written word was inadequate on its own.

You bought an expensive walking stick and appeared with it in public. One day at the Throgmorton internet café (corner Julius Nyerere and Samora Machel), you cut a sharp figure; dreadlocked, brandishing the walking stick, clad in a three piece suit and a long snuff horn protruding from your pocket. After the usual greetings you went across the intersections and walked straight to *The Mirror*. I really felt that you had arrived.

You were against one super way of viewing the spiritual. You also liked the bible, particularly the Old Testament. I remember finding you reading it in your office, explaining to a charmed colleague that God is manifest in all cultures and that the devil of the Christians is not necessarily the devil of all the non-Christians.

You wrote about biras that you had attended in Mhondoro, Nyashanu, Guruve, and even Mbare itself! In one BWAZ workshop that you conducted, it is said you knelt down and prayed to the ancestors for guidance with the workshop. All were stunned. Now people called you by your totem, 'Mhofu'. Your new found quest opened you up and gone was my 'antitotem' boy of the early 1990's. You apologised for what you had said about totems way back in 1991. I forgave you.

Then we went to Bindura to attend a Marechera commemoration one August day in 2004. It was arranged by one Ngoma of Shimmer, a policeman, and a member of the BWAZ. There were a lot of readings. There was a lot of sunshine and inspiration.

But when we decided to return to Harare that evening, a curse fell on us. It took us over seven hours to travel the 88kms between Harare and Bindura. For over four hours, we did not get a lift to Harare. We decided to hitch hike to Glendale. We hoped to get better chances there because Glendale connects Harare and Bindura, and Harare and Chiweshe. We got a few beers from the nearby shopping centre and came back to the main road. For hours on end there was not a lift for Harare! We decided to light a fire. We even went back to buy more beers and came back and rekindled our fire.

Past midnight and all the songs we had sung were exhausted. From nowhere, a spooky truck carrying cattle came along and we jumped in among the calves and the cows.

As we drove away, you looked back at our lone midnight fire and said, "I am sure he is now alone by the fire, poor man." Without asking, I knew you were referring to Marechera. Most Marechera events have a tendency to be accompanied by some mishaps, you said. I remember that when I got down at Second street shops, you continued to the city centre. You phoned an hour later saying you had got a kombi to Southerton but picked a quarrel with somebody inside there and ended up getting down and walking all the way to Southerton, and now you were not in bed but perched on a bar stool, drinking in good familiar company. I laughed and switched off.

Ruzvidzo, Free Spirit, you know too well that I have lots of respect for you.

Memory Chirere is an author and lecturer at the University of Zimbabwe. He enjoys reading and writing short stories and some of his are published in *Nomore Plastic Balls* (1999), *A Roof to Repair* (2000), *Writing Still* (2003) and *Creatures Great and Small* (2005). He has recently published the books *Somewhere in This Country* (2006), *Tudikidiki* (2007), and *Toriro and his goats* (2010).

Witch's Brew

Ruzvidzo Stanley Mupfudza

Whenever I saw the jagged pieces of a broken heart swirling in the depths of her dark soft doe-like eyes, I knew Mai Chamboko was not a witch. But many people said she was. I guess that is why there were echoes of pain in her eyes. When I asked her why her eyes were so sad, she sighed and whispered, "Ah, my little husband, perhaps it is because I yearn for understanding... and peace... things very few are willing to give."

I was her friend, though. My mother and I were the only friends Mai Chamboko had. And what was I but a club-footed child many were repulsed by even if they pretended otherwise? I understood the pain of Mai Chamboko's loneliness. I thought I knew why there were shards of her broken heart in the depths of her eyes.

Mai Chamboko had no children of her own. People called her many names. That was something that happened to me a lot. That's how I knew the shape of her heart. I saw who and what she really was —a good person, hungry only for acceptance and understanding.

I thought she was the kindest person ever. She treated me as if I had two normal feet. In fact, she made me feel as if my club-foot made me more special than any child she had ever seen.

I liked to go to her house. Many people wondered why a club-footed boy would spend so much time with a 'witch'. I loved her cooking and baking. She was always pottering around in her kitchen, humming softly. She used exotic herbs and spices whose aroma filled the air with a tangy quality that always seemed to have echoes of otherworldly tastes and magic. Ah, those cakes and scones that she used to bake — if only my taste buds could speak!

She cooked and baked, baked and cooked. There were times I thought Mai Chamboko was always preparing these

15

meals for invisible children that only she saw, who filled her empty house with the happy pitter-patter of their feet and colourful laughter that only she heard. It was as if, as far she was concerned, these children had had simply gone out to play and she expected them to burst through the door at any moment.

But, I was the only child who went to see her. None of her relatives visited her anymore. It made me sad. I think it made her even sadder, though. I don't know whether it was because many people thought her strange that an air of difference hovered around her. But then, she did not dress like many other women in the neighbourhood. She always wore loose, long, black flowing dresses. They always reminded me of priestly robes. She looked like a forlorn priestess from a forgotten sacred shrine. I later learnt that she wore black because she had never stopped mourning the death of the only child she ever bore, the one people said she had killed.

Her husband did not behave as if she had killed their child. He was a quiet man. He left in the mornings to go to work and came back in the evenings. He never said a word when the township gossips started saying he had another wife somewhere with whom he had more than six children. He simply came and went, like a shadow. Throughout the changing seasons, over the passage of time, no matter what the gossips said, he stayed with Mai Chamboko.

I think I knew why he would do that, stay with her I mean. Every time I walked through her door, Mai Chamboko's dark eyes would light up. Those shards of sadness would fade way. She would smile then. She had dusky, soft, and smooth skin. I thought she was the most beautiful woman I had ever seen. If I were her husband I would choose to live with her for the rest of my life, too. Ah, just to see those dark eyes light up and that radiant smile when it came. One day, when I saw her light up like that as I walked in, I blurted, "You are the most beautiful woman in the world."

How she glowed then.

"Ah, thank you my little husband. But tell me, where and when have you seen all the women in the world?"

"I just know it in my heart. Even if I saw a woman the whole world thought was the most beautiful, and she was not you, I would know that it was not true."

That rare radiant smile lit up her face when I said that. If only she could smile more often.

"You say some of the sweetest things ever, my little husband." She paused. "And guess what my little husband?"

"What?"

"You, my dear, are the most handsome man I know."

I beamed. She threw her head back and laughed. I liked it when Mai Chamboko laughed. Her laughter reminded of the time I had gone to the village and seen a waterfall with a spring people said was the home of water sprites. The sound of that waterfall seemed to hold a secret enchanted beauty and joy. Now that the shards of sadness had melted away from her eyes and sunlight danced in them as she laughed, I saw a Mai Chamboko those who called her a witch had shut away.

"Here, have this chocolate cake and herbal tea — it's good for the lonely heart," she said.

I smiled. That was my favourite treat, a cure for a lonely heart.

In the years things became bad in our country, when shelves in shops became barren, I wished everyone would just have her herbal tea and chocolate cake. But for many, even normal tea leaves were in short supply, and all of a sudden even chocolate cakes themselves became something many only remembered from better days. In order to make ends meet Mai Chamboko, like many women in our community, began to go to South Africa, Botswana, Namibia, and Zambia, to sell the things she crocheted and knitted. With the money she made, she would buy groceries and whatever could be used or resold back home.

The other women said she had a chikwambo or goblin, which made her successful. Stories of people who went to the dark side to find charms that would make them rich were many in our township. A chikwambo for wealth, a chikwambo for love — it seemed there was one for everything. But I didn't believe that Mai Chamboko had a money-making chikwambo. It didn't matter what I believed though.

People said Mai Chamboko had killed her child in exchange for the chikwambo. It had fed off the child's flesh and sucked her blood dry. According to them, the chikwambo had imprisoned the child's spirit in a blood-soaked gourd. This was the source of the power of the muti that made Mai Chamboko earn more money than the other women. But I didn't understand this, because the child had died long before Mai Chamboko started going on the cross-border trips.

When I asked Mai Chamboko about the rumours, she said, "There are bad men and women out there who can go to the dark side. They bring back monstrous things and make potions that are believed to bring wealth and success. But you have to shed the blood of loved ones, and sometimes even strangers. Death and blood — that is the price you have to pay. But once the chikwambo's gourd begins to run dry, it must kill. Many people see frequent deaths in their families and neighbourhoods as a result of this. The people who are killed do not really rest, for their spirits are stolen and enslaved to do this work."

I felt tears roll down my cheeks. "Why do people do such things?"

"Because they do not know any better. You see these, my little husband?" Mai Chamboko said, raising her hands, palms open. "These, your hands, your heart and mind, are all it takes to be successful. Hard work, passion, and perseverance — and nothing else. Don't let anyone ever tell you anything different."

I believed her.

So, I was not surprised that even in those lean days, there was always food in Mai Chamboko's house. This made some of the neighbours envious. They sneered behind her back, saying she did it all to please her chikwambo. After all, they said, it was not as if she had any children to feed.

She would have loved to have the house filled with children of her own. I was sure of that. I know there is nothing more she would have loved than to spoil them with her magical cooking. But after the death of her child that people said she had eaten, Mai Chamboko had not been able to have any more children. She had tried but three had been stillborn. The gossips said the babies died to give power to her goblin. This chikwambo, the people said, also enjoyed eating babies before they were born. That is why those other three had died in her womb, so the gossips said.

The other children in the township were told to stay away from Mai Chamboko's house. If they dared to go there, their parents told them, Mai Chamboko would kill them then cook and eat their flesh. Mother clicked her tongue in exasperation when I told her about the mean things people said about Mai Chamboko.

"It's all nonsense," she said. "People don't know any better."

"Even the women who go to church don't talk to her," I said.

"That's because they don't know any better. They read their bibles with closed minds and hearts. We're all God's children."

"Is that why you are still Mai Chamboko's friend?"

"We should never turn our back on one of our own who has suffered and is still in pain. She has always been my friend even if she doesn't come to church anymore. Losing her baby daughter hurt her so bad."

"Why did her baby die?" I asked.

My mother sighed and shrugged. "God knows best," she murmured. "She is not a bad person..."

I think my mother was right. Mai Chamboko was not a bad person, even if she had stopped going to church. One day as I sat on her lap, after having had chocolate cake and herbal tea, I said to her abruptly, "You know, because you are so sweet and kind, one day, you will have another beautiful baby girl."

She pulled back her head and looked at me closely. "Why do you say that, my little husband?"

"Because we are all God's children."

"Ah, my sweet little husband, how true. But God seems to have laughed at me."

She looked past me into space, to a distant time where painful things roamed.

"God knows best," I said.

She smiled and said, "How true, my little husband."

"One day, you shall have the peace you desire."

"I don't know... the years of pain and loneliness have been too long..."

"Don't worry," I said softly. "I've seen a child and heard the sound of this child's laughter in this house."

"Do you mean the one the hungry earth claimed so early, my little husband?"

"No," I said. "The one still to come."

She looked at me intently. She knew me better than many people. "If only it could be so." She sighed.

I smiled knowingly. "It will be so. It is written. Just keep on knitting, cooking and being kind like your grandmother," I said.

She gave a little start. "My little husband, how do you know about my grandmother? I don't believe I have ever told you about her, have I?"

I shrugged. I could never explain how I knew some of these things. It happened a lot. In a flash, I would suddenly see and know things. In a moment, a vision so clear I could almost touch it would come to me and I would know about something or someone. It was this gift — which many thought a curse — and my club-foot, which made very few

20

other children want to play with me. They called me 'Creepy Clubby'. But Mai Chamboko said everything I had was a gift and it made me precious. Now, after I had mentioned her grandmother, she became wistful.

"She was a healer you know, my grandmother," Mai Chamboko said. "But lonely and an outcast. Everyone said she was a witch. My people say that her spirit follows me and that is why I cannot have children any more."

"She wasn't a witch," I said. "And neither are you."

For a moment, those distant clouds of sorrow that hovered in her eyes faded away as she smiled that rare brilliant smile of hers. "You are a strange one my little husband, but in a good and special way. You are truly blessed. You are precious, my little husband."

I beamed and squeezed her hand affectionately.

There were times, though, I wished people would see me the way Mai Chamboko did. I remember clearly how people had started thinking I was evil. It all began that day I begged the township perennial drunk, Baba Praise, whom everyone called Baba Pure, not to go in search of the illicit kachasu brew that was sold in the woodlands near the polluted river that ran through the veldt at the edge of the township.

"Baba Pure, Baba Pure, please don't go there today," I begged him, weeping, tugging at his 'work-suit'. That is what he called the faded blue overalls he always wore when he was going drinking, which was all the time. It so happened that that night, a fight broke out among the beer drinkers. In that fight Baba Praise was stabbed to death. The quarrel had been something about money, a small amount, but the cost had been his life. The details were hazy but the only clear thing was that Baba Praise died.

People said I had put a curse on him. I had not. All I know is that when I had looked at him, that day, I had seen a white shroud draped around his body instead of the 'work-suit' he wore. I had only seen what I had seen. On seeing that vision, I had felt a terrible dread sip from my heart and course through my body like a cold chill, which I could not explain to him or anyone. How I wished I was all grown up and had words with which to speak to people so that they could understand these things that I saw and felt.

So because I did not have the words the people made up their own words about me. The fact that I spent so much time with Mai Chamboko did nothing to dispel the rumours of witchcraft and curses. The people said she was tutoring me so that I would take over after she was dead. After all, they said, she had no child of her own and the craft needed to be passed on. A witchcraft apprentice, me?

I don't know how people could think and believe this or that Mai Chamboko had killed her only child and eaten the tender flesh. But, they said, children and babies were a favourite delicacy among witches. But how could a woman who knitted so well and baked such scrumptious cakes that made every day seem like my birthday, be a witch? I think it was because they avoided her and hardly spoke to her that they said these things. I loved her company and the things she said.

One day, she said to me, "Do you know, my little husband, children like you come from a special place where magic and miracles bring sunshine to lives of everyone around them? There, people judge not according to how you look, but according to the shape and nature of your heart."

I sighed. I believed her.

"How I wish the people here would make that place possible in our midst, too," she said.

I squeezed her hand.

Sometimes, when I was not in her kitchen, I would take solitary walks through the township streets. I loved it because then I could see the ghostly beings that no one else saw. There are some things that walk in our midst, which would mortify many if they had the eyes with which to see. I think God was kind enough to make most blind to them. But just because they couldn't see them didn't mean that

22

these creatures did not brush shoulders with the living. Ah, these people who thought they knew it all, and yet were oblivious to a whole world in the middle of their own. Yes, if they had had eyes with which to see some of the monsters that walked in our midst they would have been terrified to death for sure. I think they could not see because darker monsters walked in their own minds and hearts. The ugliness inside them made their eyes blind to everything else around them, even the beauty that could be found in our overcrowded township.

You see, I think when our country had crumbled and everything was decaying all around us, there came a time when people only saw the mountains of uncollected garbage. There was also the litany of broken sewer pipes, which gushed torrents of raw sewage into streets and homes. The road had mega-potholes and we ended up having ponds, giving a whole new meaning to township cesspools. The decaying garbage and the stench from the broken sewer pipes sang hymns of rot to whose rhythms many souls moved. So, in the end, the magic that wafted from Mai Chamboko's kitchen was lost on them.

I was thinking of these things as I walked slowly through the township streets one day. As always, these walks gave time to think deep thoughts, some of which when I told my mother would make her sigh and say, "You have the soul of an ancient man." But my mother said this not unkindly. I smiled when I thought of this and how she was like Mai Chamboko, seeing me for who I really was, not judging me because of the way I looked.

My thoughts came to an abrupt end when I heard someone snarl: "Hey Creepy Clubby, where are you off to with Nick Price's golf club?"

There were sniggers. My eyes abruptly moved away from the winged human butterfly that was flying by, and rested on the boy who was standing in front of me. I had been so wrapped up in my thoughts and that other world, I had not seen him and his cronies walk up to me. He was no butterfly. More like a wasp whose nest had been disturbed. I knew him, and with him, every living thing in his path disturbed his nest by simply existing. The other boys seemed quite at home amidst the rubbish and stench on this particular stretch of the street. They watched us gleefully. Quite clearly, it had been a dreary day for them thus far. I said nothing.

"Always mighty uppity aren't we, going with our nose in the air!" snarled the boy again.

His eyes were hard. I knew that stones rattled in the place where his heart ought to have been. Somewhere in the depths inside him, a trapped happy soul had given up trying to come out. Everyone called him Tyson, because he liked to fight at the slightest excuse. He was in his early teens, but his face was so pinched with a perpetual sneer that he looked like an old man with a penchant for going through life with a lemon clenched between his teeth. There was so much anger coiled inside him.

"God made a mistake by making you come into our world half-formed and unfinished like this."

I said nothing.

"In the old days, you would have been killed at birth because children like you are bad luck," he snarled.

I looked at him quietly.

"So where's your witch-bitch wife, out and about riding her hyena, heh?"

The sniggers grew louder. I held my peace.

"Why, you must be a hyena-child yourself, huh, Creepy Clubby?" he said, and came closer.

I recoiled. Tyson's breath smelt no better than the rotting garbage and putrid water gushing out of the sewer pipes around us. It seemed like a gut rot — something that rose from the pit of his stomach where, apparently, his heart had fallen, shattered, died, and was rotting away.

"Tell us, Creepy Clubby, is it true old man Chamboko is getting it on the side? He doesn't do it anymore with his witch of a wife, huh? Maybe you are giving it to her instead, hmm? So what's it like? A club-footed freak and witch doing it, what's that like, huh?"

A rock hard finger jabbed me in the chest. I staggered and tottered to the ground. Jeers and applause filled the air. Tyson grinned.

"Why all that human meat you are always cooking with those hideous spices you use to disguise the smell of cooking flesh hasn't made you strong, has it? Puny as a reed aren't you?"

Tyson was quite clearly entering an ecstatic nirvana where people like him thrived. I looked up at him. In that instant I saw an eagle and viper fighting. The eagle's talons clutched the shredded bleeding snake as the bird triumphantly flew to its nest at the top of a mountain.

"If you go to suburbs to steal again tonight you shall not return," I said quietly.

There was a stunned silence as his gang gaped at me. Tyson's face became ashen for a while and then he kicked me viciously.

"Shut up you circus freak. You think you can scare me with one of your curses, huh?"

"Hey, Blah Ty," said one of his cronies, pulling him away, "let him be. Let's get away from here."

The rest of the gang murmured their consent. He cast me one last murderous glance and allowed himself to be pulled away.

"Strange kid, how did he know our plans?" I heard one of the boys whisper fearfully.

"Rubbish, he knows nothing," hissed Tyson.

Everyone in the township knew that Tyson and his gang were behind many break-ins and muggings in the neighbourhood. When the police harassed them, they had started to hunt further afield. Everyone knew this. Yet the gang never seemed to get arrested. There had been a time once or twice, yes, when they had been detained for a day or two. Then they were soon seen sauntering down the streets again and the elders in the township shook their heads, muttering, "The police of today! All they want is chemusana!" That was what people called bribes. Work was supposed to be back-breaking and therefore one needed compensation. Since salaries were inadequate many felt that that compensation had to be found from other means, like bribes. That was just the way it was, in a place where sewers burst freely from the rusty pipes and gushed joyously down the streets, while a chorus of flies sang hymns and praises from pool to pool, house to house, like fervent Pentecostal evangelists hungry for souls to save. Disease was only a fly away. Besides, there were very few souls being saved here, many were more than willing to be bought and sold. Ndizvo zviripo, they said.

Anyway, the likes of Tyson and his gang believed that if our politicians could get away with lying, cheating, stealing and killing, so could they. So that night, despite my warnings, they went on another escapade. We heard the news of the fatal shooting the next day. Tyson's gang had tried to break into a house in an upmarket northern suburb around seven in the evening. The home-owner had been armed. When he heard sounds of an attempted entry he had shouted a warning, which was ignored, and he had fired. Tyson was the only casualty. He made the front-page of the only daily paper. The gang was believed to have been part of a ring that had been terrorising neighbourhoods lately.

When I heard the news, people had already started gathering at Tyson's family's house for the funeral. Among our people there is a saying wafa wanaka, which means that when someone passes away, whatever evil or bad things they committed in life are temporarily forgotten during the funeral and mourning period. In public, no one speaks ill of the dead. So even the most notorious of thugs could count on a pretty good attendance of family and neighbours during their wake. It was no different for Tyson. But whispers about my 'curse' started doing the rounds.

The house where Tyson's family lived was dilapidated. Nothing grew in the yard. Tyson's father had gone to South Africa one year in search of opportunities that our country no longer had. He promised to send money and groceries once he got something going down South. The money and groceries never came. He was never heard from and of again. Tyson's mother started going to the township tavern. Many men started calling at the house. None of Tyson's brothers and sisters — some of whom had been born long after Tyson's father had taken the gap — worked. Not surprisingly, on the day of the funeral there wasn't enough food to feed the neighbours. In our community, people will come to mourn the dead, whether out of sincerity or not. They feel duty bound to do this, particularly the neighbours. Tyson was Mai Chamboko's and our neighbour. In times of hunger, funerals can be a good opportunity to get something into the belly.

Tyson's mother muttered, "How am I going to feed all these people? That good for nothing boy, causing me nothing but headaches in life and death."

There was an uneasy silence.

"I can help."

There were startled murmurs. The offer had come from Mai Chamboko. There had been discomfort among the mourners when she had arrived to pass her condolences. But this was a funeral — it brought together even long-warring enemies. Besides, Mai Chamboko was a neighbour and there was nothing they could do but accept her in their midst. However, that discomfort returned to the surface when she made her offer. But there was an inescapable fact, they were hungry.

"Wafa wanaka," my mother said quietly.

I wondered if she was referring to Tyson or was using the term to mean something else here. Thankfully, Tyson's mother was not a woman to hold grudges against anyone anyway. Besides, she knew the burden of being an outcast. Being a prostitute among neighbours who went either to

27

Pentecostal, traditional, and mapositori churches— each according to the way the spirit moved them — was not easy. Once she made up her mind, she regarded prostitution as the only way she could fend for herself and her children after her husband's abandonment. She had shrugged and said, "The tavern is my temple."

Although she had never gone out of her way to befriend Mai Chamboko, now, in the wake of her offer, she said, "Look, I don't care one way or the other what she does in her spare time. She has never interfered with my affairs, and if she says she will help then let her. Any objections?"

There did not seem to be any.

No one left. In the end, everyone said it was the best funeral they had ever attended. No one could say exactly what it was about the food that Mai Chamboko and the other women cooked around the funeral fire that day. In fact, no one could say that Mai Chamboko bewitched him or her because she was cooking in full view of the other women who were helping her. Besides, she ate the food too. It was customary at funerals to simply boil cabbages — tomatoes and onions were a luxury — and cook sadza in a big drum and then serve the people. Culinary skills were not expected or required, just that everyone present ate. To be certain, Mai Chamboko cooked in a big drum to feed all the people present. Yet that sadza, those cabbages and that funeral were simply magical. When people asked, Mai Chamboko simply shrugged and said she had put her heart into the cooking; she knew the pain of losing a child.

It was also that night, at that funeral for a boy who had brought misery to everyone around him, that many found ecstasy through song and dance. They rediscovered, too, what a powerful and beautiful singer Mai Chamboko was. We have always been a people who sing and dance at both happy and sad occasions. Singing and dancing brings us closer together and in times of grief lightens the burden. During funerals the curtains are removed from windows of the sitting room where the women gather and sing songs.

The men sit outside, on the veranda and the open space leading to the front gate. At night they start a fire, which they sit around, talking and even laughing while the women sing and dance inside.

That night, when Mai Chamboko broke into song, those who had gone to church with her before her child died suddenly remembered that back then they had believed angels descended from heaven whenever she sang. But it was not just the church songs that she sang that night, for she led, too, in some traditional songs that many had forgotten. Since Tyson's mother also had friends with whom she fraternised in the course of her work, it wasn't a hundred percent pious gathering; the sacred and secular intermingled freely that night.

In fact, I remember that when I looked through the curtain-less window, it was one of Tyson's mother's friends, a dark-complexioned woman who took over the beating of the drum when Mai Chamboko broke into Mbire; an old song about death and the return to the mountains, the final resting place of all souls: Kuenda Mbire, waenda chose/Kusara mugomo wa wega wega — When you go to Mbire, you go forever/Your soul remains alone in the mountains. The song goes back to the time of our forebears, who founded our great nation, who were known as Masters of the Land, and were associated with the mountains and with hunting and tilling the land. Mbire was their original homeland, and when they had come to this country they had seen a mountain that reminded them of a similar one in Mbire, and so they had called it Mbire too. It was a sacred mountain imbued with mythical currents and was a gateway to the home of spirits. If Jesus said his father's mansion had many rooms, perhaps to my forebears, Mbire was one such room, where souls returned once the flesh had ceased to be. I wondered if Tyson's soul belonged there.

But seeing prostitutes and members of the Gracious Women from the various denominations mingling was a stark reminder of why our funerals can house a terrible beauty. Death can bring the most unlikely people together, rekindling ancient memories and bonds. So that night the woman from the bar played the drum as if possessed, forcing many onto their feet and dancing fervently. It was then in the midst of dance and song that Mai Chamboko broke into tears, but her voice grew stronger and sweeter and everyone agreed they had never seen or heard anything like it before. Afterwards, Tyson's mother broke into tears too. When the song came to an end she hugged Mai Chamboko. One by one, all the other women came and hugged her too.

I heard mother say, "We are all God's children."

I sighed and looked across the fire around at where Mai Chamboko's husband sat from where he could see into the house. I stood up and walked to him and sat beside him. He had listened to his wife sing and I saw something glisten in his eyes. I reached out for his hand and said, "God knows best."

Something happened that night that no one has been able to explain ever since. But we all know that after that funeral a good number of the women began to visit Mai Chamboko, who taught them knitting, embroidery, and new recipes. They joined forces and started going across the border as a team. When the shortages that bedevilled our country grew worse, it was the women led by Mai Chamboko who kept our community going.

A few months after that funeral she stopped wearing black robes. It was then that everyone noticed that Mai Chamboko's belly was growing bigger and bigger. I walked into Mai Chamboko's kitchen and her face lit up, "Ah, my little husband," she said and hugged me. I smiled, caressing her belly. We were not witches, Mai Chamboko and I.

Born in Zimbabwe in 1971, Ruzvidzo Stanley Mupfudza developed a passion for the art of story telling and a love for the written word at a tender age. Long before he was literate he would gaze with fascination at the beauty of the written word on scraps of paper, old magazines, newspapers, books, et al, and by the time he was in the third grade was a passionate wide reader, whose reading material was more often than not way beyond his scope.

It was also at this time that he started writing his own stories, spurred by a vivid imagination and his already entrenched reading culture. After studying Literature in English at the University of Zimbabwe, he worked, for eight years, as a high school English Language and Literature in English teacher before moving to Zimbabwe's national television broadcaster where he worked as Chief Producer of Social and Cultural programmes for children. After that spell, his perennial wanderlust saw him move on to the world of advertising, where he worked as a copywriter for a local advertising agency.

It was not long before he packed his creative bags and joined the mainstream print media as an Assistant Editor, specialising in feature writing and covering the arts for a Zimbabwean daily and weekly paper. He eventually became the Acting Editor of the weekly Sunday paper until its demise in 2007. There was a particularly rough patch where he survived through the benevolence of friends, his art and freelancing. In 2008 he returned to the world of advertising.

His poetry, essays and short stories have been published in Zimbabwe and abroad. His early poetry started appearing in the University of Zimbabwe English Department's literary magazine, *The Bloom*, and national and international magazines. His stories appear in the following anthologies, *A Roof to Repair* (Harare: College Press), *Creatures Great and Small* (Gweru: Mambo Press 2000), *Writing Still: New Stories from Zimbabwe* (Harare: Weaver Press, 2003), *Writing Now: More Stories from*

Zimbabwe (Harare: Weaver Press, 2005), and *Dreams, Miracles and Jazz: New Adventures in African Writing* (Northlands: Picador Africa, 2008). A revised version of his story, "The Mender of Broken Soles" has been published online by SABLE Literary Magazine. He has also been interviewed on Conversations with Writers and Kubatana.net, and also occasionally, when the spirit moved him, blogged at Zimbablog

Ruzvidzo passed away on the 3rd of May 2010. He will be missed, a great loss for Literature and Zimbabwe; may his works live on in our hearts and minds forever.

Main

NoViolet Bulawayo

Main. Main Street standing up straight and adjusting the rainbow-coloured wrap skirt that threatens to slide down her wide waist, black blood boiling in her veins. Bustling throbbing writhing street. Everything moving: cars, voices, ambitions, money, dreams, feet, smoke. Just moving moving moving — like a wind.

The thin reed of a woman in the screaming red dress, the one carrying a black bundle in her arms, suddenly pauses right in the centre of Main Street and thrusts her chest out in pain. She twists her neck and tilts her small head, flipping the long, brown hair that is not hers. Next, she half-raises a stockinged left leg, deliberately, like she not only needs to place it somewhere, but on a somewhere that is better than any somewhere she has ever stood.

Her scarecrow arms extend outward, away from her body, but she still holds on to the black bundle. No, she does not wish to drop it; she will hold on to it. Hold tight, tighter. The pain in her heart is a frantic, frenzied drumbeat. Slightly stiffening, she can feel her chest first reeling, then crowding, then heaving inward, but still, she will not drop her bundle; it is the only thing she owns. For a moment, she stands balancing on the sole-less heel of a small green shoe, balancing dangerously but also gracefully as if she weighs nothing more than a folded whisper.

When her body eventually slams into the concrete it is like a careful dance coming to an end. Her black bundle rolls like a coin and rests in a nearby dirty gutter, right across from the blind woman in the black dress and white hat who sings for a living, her fierce voice not stopping once for anything that happens on Main Street, singing:

"Tshiya lumhlaba lentozawo,

Thabathisphambano ulandele,

Ngcono ngiz'hambele ngalindlela,

33

Tshiya lumhlaba lentozawo."

The crowd that gathers around the fallen woman swells and swells like a flooding river. Within minutes the river swallows the woman so that with all those writhing bodies looming above her, she looks like a stain. The onlookers do not see the woman's fallen bundle; it suits them better to only see her, especially because she is dead. There are details to be taken in and notes to be made before someone comes and moves the body. And since later, at a yet-to-come time, the dead woman on Main Street will be born again in their mouths, in a story; this is exactly the moment to gather that story.

First they have to take in the material of the red dress (Georgette — and frayed), the half-undone hem held by a thread (white), the hint of a petticoat peeping underneath the dress (yellow and dirty), the green shoes with the soles worn and the nail of one heel showing (old, made in China), the brown weave with the strange streaks (cheap), a faint smell coming from somewhere (definitely not perfume — foul), and the bitten, painted fingernails (red — to go with the rather big lips and dress).

If the woman's heart could also be seen it surely would look no better than her beggarly dress; it is sick and diseased; swollen. Death carried in the chest. Perhaps better they cannot see the heart — and the woman's other innards for that matter — perhaps it's better that they see only the outside of her. And as for that outside — well, anybody who has eyes can tell the woman is poor, a nobody. The crowd knows the death of a nobody is not really worth seeing, not worth stopping for.

The knowledge is unspoken but understood by all — they should have just kept on to their destinations. With deaths that happen on the street you really have to be careful with your time, the way you would with money. You can't be stopping to watch every single one. They know there are better deaths. Somewhere where the victims are at least worth looking at. Better spectacles in other places; after all, there are other streets besides Main. Many other streets.

Main. Main Street adjusting her black, faded push-up bra so she holds everything together — the police, the expectations, the boiling cars, the weary buildings, the dirt, the broken dreams, the falling dollar, the billions of worthless money, the queues-Jesus-Jesus-Jesus the queues. Every day they leave their homes and descend on Main like prodigal birds after a battering flight, firmly plant their fatigued feet on the street and wait.

They stand one after the other, packed tight like ants, like powder, like bricks, the body angled upright, arms crossed at the chest, or akimbo, feet slightly apart — this, they now know after enough years of doing it, is the proper way to stand in a queue. They have become a people of queues, every time a time of queues, every day a day of queues: queues for water, food, medical attention, transport, queues for whatever else they need to stay alive.

Waiting in one queue they let their eyes dart down the length of Main's long spine, settling only briefly on the dirty windows of empty shops that can no longer afford to stay in business, on the crumpled face of the old woman who wobbles like a drunk from the queue and props herself against a leafless jacaranda tree — dizzy and unable to stand any longer, on the old, peeling statue of the country's president, on the policemen waiting in squads on Robert Mugabe Way and brandishing batons and handcuffs and guns.

Once they take all this in, they shift their weight from one foot to the other so they do not stress the legs and the body; somehow the legs and body have to survive this queue just so they can join the next queue, and the next, and the next. They run discoloured tongues lightly along their chapped lips — standing for hours in a queue, in the searing sun, will indeed dry one's lips. They swallow dry saliva with the reed-thin hope of silencing their grumbling bellies —

one tends to get really hungry waiting on an empty stomach.

Then they look at the tall teenager in the yellow T-shirt that spells Obama for Change, the one who has been obsessively checking his watch with restless eyes. They see him finally relax his tense poise as he reaches the front of the queue. When he gets to the cashier, they hear him politely asking, in a voice quivering with desperation, to be allowed to take out more than the Z$100 million dollars that is the daily withdrawal limit. He says his father is sick with the cholera that is killing many, and he badly needs medication.

When the boy's request is denied he pleads, and then he begs, his voice hollow and subdued with anxiety. When he is denied still, his desperation flicks like a red switch and turns to the most glaring outrage. The boy shouts his anger at the bank teller, his once smothered voice now hot and burning, now a voice to scald skins; it rises like steam and spills onto Main.

The voice only lives the short, bright life of a lighted matchstick; the police explode from the street and descend onto the boy, promptly putting out the burning match. It rains slaps, batons, screams, thrashing, punches, kicks, pounding, blood, and more blood. When the police are done, the boy resembles a wet, red rag. They put him in handcuffs before dragging him away like a dead cat.

The queue stays intact; they do not move from it to stop the beating. No. When it is over they look at the now red boy from the broken windows in their eyes and say nothing, silently reproaching his stupidity in thinking he had a freedom of expression, a right to vomit his outrage right there on the street in front of everybody. He must learn to control it if he wants to live, to hide it the way women once tucked fifty dollar bills in their bras way back when a fifty dollar bill could fit inside a woman's bra, back when women could still afford bras.

They too know outrage; they are outraged to be standing in the unending queues; outraged to be billionaires who cannot afford to feed themselves and their families; outraged at the life that is becoming unliveable; outraged at the police standing on Main and everywhere else to squash them like cockroaches if they dare protest the state of things; outraged at some people they won't name, for failing the country. Their outrage throbs like a salted wound but they hold it inside; they know of many who have dared show it like the boy and got exactly what he got, and in some cases, worse. They do not want that for themselves, no thank you, they do not — better anything, better they stand here queuing on Main.

Main. Main Street holds them, but just briefly. There is no time for loving. She ducks behind a corner to wipe the sweat collected under her breasts, on her stomach, between her thighs. When she sees the horde coming she tosses her damp handkerchief, bites her bottom lip, and braces herself once more.

NoViolet Bulawayo considers herself a storyteller first, and a writer second. She completed her MFA in fiction at Cornell University. Her short story, 'Snapshots', was a finalist for the 2009 SA PEN/Studzinski Literary Award, and she won the 2011 Caine Prize with 'Hitting Budapest'.

A Writer's Lot

Zukiswa Wanner

So here I am in Sun City. I could tell you about all of the journalists in my sleep, but I won't. Well, not a lot. I would rather tell you about the one who landed me here.

It always began with emails.

"Dear Mr. Dube,

I am a journalist from *New York Times* / *Times* / *Newsweek* / *Le Monde* / *The Guardian*," etcetera, etcetera. Then there are the flattering platitudes about how the journalist loves my first work of fiction, *Township Stories*. And then, inevitably it ends, "I will be in Johannesburg from _____ to _____ and would love to interview you as one of the literary torchbearers in post-apartheid South Africa."

Sometimes it would be a male journalist. Most of the time she would be female, trying to understand how I survived 'growing up under apartheid' and trying to show me and the rest of their readers in the Global North just how liberal they are. "There is this absolutely awesome South African writer, Sifiso Dube, you should read him," trying to sound more knowledgeable than the people around them at a dinner party. When it was a female journalist, there would be sex. It seemed inevitable — the price I paid, or the prize I received, depending really on how good the sex was, for fame.

And that's just it Joe. When I set out to write *Township Stories*, I was a township boy, a Wits dropout, who never imagined the book would get as big as it has. Of course it is every writer's fantasy to be published, but at the most, I thought it might be read in Cape Town. Never thought it would go international, let alone be translated in all the major UN languages. Eish. It was a boost to a man's ego.

But then, amajita see you emapepeni, on TV, hear you on radio and they think wena u grootman. They don't understand that at this point in time, five months after your book has been published, you have not received your first royalty cheque yet. If you are lucky, as I was, you immediately get some freelance gigs with some papers reviewing books because suddenly the fuckers who would never have employed you as a receptionist think you are the man. You get a little change in your pocket and you know what? You find yourself playing the part of the big man that your boys think you are.

I can't tell majimbos kuthi just because they saw me on TV yesterday, the hundred rand that I have in my pocket is the last money I have and so, I buy a round or two, then I feign tiredness and walk to Carlton Centre to take one of those illegal taxis that have ten of you in a six-seater for ten rand each to ferry you elokshin. No, I am not still staying with my mother, who do you think I am? In keeping up with my supposed status, I have been renting a cottage in the hip Melville since I became famous but when it's late and I am in Newtown (the artists' haven), I always find myself travelling to my mother's house in Pimville. It's cheaper than the sixty rand I would have to pay otherwise.

The better part of the fame, of course, is amacherrie who suddenly want to know me. Particularly, the reading Model C types who would never have looked at me twice when I passed them before. I see them come up to me and say, "I just wanted to say Sifiso (this type never ghettoise your name and call you Fistos), your book really moved me. I have a cousin/uncle/ half-brother/step-brother (never brother) who is so like your protagonist," before they give you some lame excuse to give you their number. Generally it is the old and lame, "I am also a writer and I would like you to read my manuscript," although I never got to see most of the said manuscripts. Before I know it, I find myself screwing this hot woman whom I never thought I could have in my wildest dreams. Soon I get tired of them though because they always want to be the protagonist in my next book/novella/short story, or, at the least, that I should give them a shout out in my next book. Because of the literary groupies and the number of women I have shagged since my book came out, I have begun to think of myself as the thinking groupies' kwaito star or house DJ. I know I get as much play with women as any kwaito or house singer you could name, only with me, I'm actually getting intelligent women not the video groupies.

But back to the international journalists.

What I didn't bargain for was the intellectual exploitation I would get from them. Sonny! At first I dug it. What better way to publicise my book? Write a short story for us, do an interview — but eventually I saw through it.

I was being exploited. They would do interviews and earn megabucks selling the story of who they think I am. They would ask me for a short story, and I, bloody excitable fool that I was, excited that I was getting an international platform, would write it and never ask for payment, or when I got payment, it would be measly while they got rich off the sweat of my brow — or mind. They would come and ask me, for no pay, "Can you give us a tour to Soweto?" and I would do it man. Do it thinking it was part of the interview and would help my stature but I would not get a penny for my time — well, save for the free drinks when I meet a kindred spirit in alcohol in the form of a journo. I am a writer first above all else of course but what these international journalists don't understand (and never enquire about) is that, unlike my European counterparts, the South African government department responsible for art does not pay writers (or any other artists in general) to do what they are good at. So, if I am not freelancing and I am still six months away from my royalty cheque, I do not eat.

Talking about royalty cheques, publishers really have a talent for screwing first time writers in the arse. When my publisher told me my book was going for a reprint after just three months, I was ecstatic. Three months later when I received my first royalty cheque, I cried. I am considering asking some parliamentarian to write a constitutional amendment so that the definition of rape can include what publishers do to writers' intellectual property by way of books. Some of these motherfuckers should be rotting in jail for such gross violation of my drinking money.

But I digress. So three months ago I get an email from a journalist for some Scandinavian paper. He tells me he is coming to South Africa, would like to do an interview with me wara wara and I should give him a tour of Soweto because he has 'always followed South African politics, Mandela is my role model, and I think it's a shame what happened to your people with the forced removals in Sophiatown. I am also impressed with the way you bring the South African township to reality and would love to get a tour of Soweto with you.' I am already well-known all over the country by people who matter and I know I should pull a JM Coetzee and say 'I don't do interviews' but I respond and say, "Yeah. I can do that." Fame is a terrible thing Joe. It gets into a man's head.

Of course I start laughing after reading the email because I think to myself, damn these motherfuckers. Why do they always have to exhort Mandela's name in all things South African? And of course I am equally amused by the whole Sophiatown bullshit. Goddammit, it was twenty years before I was born!

But alright. I tell myself that this punk has to pay me. I am done with being a free tour guide for these Western journalists. You want a tour of Soweto, go to Gauteng Tourism Authority and get a tour and pay for it like everyone else, otherwise — pay me, motherfucker, pay me! These fools don't understand that I have two children to look after and I don't have a steady income. And yes, before you ask, the children have two different mothers. One was an honest-to-the-gods-and-ancestors mistake and the other one, well, I think the bitch just wanted to trap me because she saw I was going places. But I do my bit, you know. When I have iclipper or two, I will drink sixty percent and divide the remains between the two children. I try to be a good father. I think I am a better father than most, which, if you know the brotherhood of fathers in my hood, or Sperm Donors as the bitter ex's like to call us, is not saying much but it's still something.

Anyway, back to this Scandinavian journo, Marcus, who has landed me in this place. He arrives in Johannesburg and we agree to meet. He has a rented car. I ask him how much he's going to pay me for the tour in a jocular tone — though I am serious as the proverbial heart attack. He tells me he can't pay me anything except for food and drinks incurred during the course of our journey because he has no money. He has a beautiful Konica camera though, so I get on my cell to my boys ekasi and tell them all about it.

"We'll pass by The Rock around eleven in the evening," I tell them in tsotsitaal with the victim looking on uncomprehendingly and smiling foolishly, in the way of an ethnographer who attempts to be comfortable with any and all different surroundings. And there and then, my boys and I have set into motion a plan to relieve him of all the money he claims not to have. I was sick and tired of starving while these punks stayed in five star hotels all under pretext of coming to interview me, while not even caring whether I had a five cent piece (Yeah that one. Y'know the one that the Department of Finance claim is still legal tender but the taxi drivers won't take?). Tonight, or that night, was going to be the day of reckoning. I asked him to pick me up at six.

He seemed a little doubtful.

"Wouldn't it be better if we travelled during the day?" Marcus asked with a little uncertainty in his voice.

I shrugged and gave him the if-you-are-too-chicken speech, "Soweto actually comes alive after seven because everyone works during the day, but if you would rather go during the day..." I left the sentence hanging while shrugging my shoulders again.

He jumped to the bait like I knew he would, wanting to show me the face of a fearless white man. See, we were two men. A black African man and a white European man and he thought he could read my mind. That white people are too scared to confront black people in their own backyard. He feared, because he had read it in my book, that as a black man I thought that he would not be able to hang, that he was a victim of the swaart gevaar tactics as espoused by the white South African expatriates that may have run to his country.

"No it's cool, we go in the evening. I pick you at six yeah?" he answered, trying to sound suave with deeply accented English — although of course, the same could be said for me, when I speak, by the Anglo-Saxons.

Marcus arrived at six on the dot; I wondered whether he had never heard of African time. I was not dressed yet although I had showered. He waited while I picked some clothes that would not make him feel too intimidated, but that would make me fit in when I got back to the hood — my Pirates cap, a hoodie, a pair of jeans and of course, my All-Star takkies.

I took him on a circuitous route via Soweto Highway. We made a stop for dinner at Nambitha, just so that he could see a few white people on tour buses and not feel too out of place. He was drinking Black Labels as per my advice. After dinner, we hung out at one or two shebeens in Dube. He drank some more while I sipped slowly as I got in conversation with people around me. By the time we got to The Rock at eleven, he was sloshed and driving erratically. I on the other hand, was still alright. I had been downing Castle Lites — guess SABMiller were right when they said that's the one to have 'when having more than one'. As we pulled in at The Rock, my boys came by with some toy guns probably taken from their children at home.

"White man. And you, cheese boy, give us your wallet or we shoot."

Marcus, in his drunken haze asks, "Are we being robbed?"

I nod my head and say, "Better do as they say otherwise they will kill us."

I hand over my wallet and cell to one of my boys, and then in fear, Marcus does the same.

"Your camera back there?" one of my boys asks.

I let Marcus lean, pick it from the back seat and pass it on. All the time I keep saying, "Eish," like I cannot believe this is happening to me and I am in shock.

When they leave us Marcus looks at me and questions, "I thought you said we would be alright." He is disillusioned. He thought he was travelling with one of the township legends and here he is robbed of all his euros and his Konica camera.

I shake my head and say, "Eish, who knew? I'm so sorry Marcus. I have come here so many times and this has never happened. In fact, just last week I was here with X of Times magazine," I say, name dropping to show how this is truly a first-time experience for me. "But you know what, to be safe, we'll have to go to a police station in Melville or in town because if we use one this side, when we come out of the police station, some other crooks may have taken your tyres."

The reality hits him. Hard. He sobers up. And he is on a fast track to town. I direct him to John Vorster Square.

I should not have, of course. I was a fool to do that. Every South African knows that the police are only vigilant when the victim is white and ultra vigilant when the victim is a white tourist. The police may just be fools with matric but they know where their government's foreign aid comes from. Not too long after, one of my boys was caught by an undercover policeman who he thought was a Nigerian, trying to sell Marcus's passport. Just what idiot would do that? Marcus's wallet had two thousand euros in traveller's cheques and some change. With my passport, I could have changed that at the nearest bank as a gift and the three of us would have had many booze-induced sleeps, but no, the retard had to get greedy. And then, as if that were not bad enough, this fool, when he got caught, spewed all the beans and identified me as the mastermind. This, before I had even changed the euros. One wonders, is there no honour among thieves any more?

The good news, of course, is that, the day after the robbery, my two partners had come to give me the traveller's cheques to change. I am the only one who knows where they are.

In a year's time, when I get out of Sun City, as the locals have nicknamed this prison, I am going to change those euros. I hope to high heavens the rand isn't too powerful by then. Meanwhile, I write my stories and look over my shoulder hoping that none of the 26 gang decides to make me their bitch.

I have a feeling, when I get out, that any book I write will be a bestseller — this place has given me plenty of ideas — and besides, South Africa and the world love former jailbirds. Isn't that what Mandela is all about?

I sit in Sun City.

Write.

And bide my time.

Zukiswa Wanner is author of the novels: *The Madams*, *Behind Every Successful Man*, and *Men of the South*. She has contributed short stories to a few anthologies. Wanner is one of the founding members of the literacy initiative, Read SA, and famous for having been short-listed for many literary awards but never winning. She does not like pina collada or getting caught in the rain. In fact, if she had control of these things, rain would only fall on farms (you too would feel this way if you had ever been caught in a Johannesburg thunderstorm). When she told her mother that she had decided to become a full time writer her mother's response was, 'most people learn to write in first grade, why can't you move on to greater things?' Her mother now thinks she is the best writer worldwide, even better than the Adichies' daughter.

Longing for Home

Hajira Amla

Grace Chirima's hard black boots crunched on the frozen ground below her. Breathing clouds of steam, she clutched her coat tighter as she walked through the shortcut next to the old church. At least it wasn't raining today.

I wonder what the weather is like back home today, she pondered. Would the tomatoes be ready to pick yet? It would still be a little longer before the maize could be harvested. All the children would want to carry the watering cans, because it would mean that they could splash a little water on each other when Mhamha wasn't looking. On hot days it was worth the risk of getting a scolding.

Grace reached the entrance of Harrow-on-the-Hill station. She touched her blue Oyster card onto the reader and hurried through the turnstile.

A bored, tinny voice echoed through the stairwell as Grace descended to Platform Three. "Ladies and gentlemen, there will be a 15-minute delay on all trains due to ice on the tracks. Please be careful of ice patches on the platforms. Thank you."

She would probably have to stand for the full hour's journey on the train. And she would be late for work. She walked up to the very end of the platform, the rough salt crunching underfoot. The platform was already pushed for standing-room and it was imperative for a small person like Grace to try and work out where the doors of the train would be once it came to a halt. Being shoved unceremoniously into the train from all sides was better than trying to find a way to squeeze in from an angle.

December in Zimbabwe was always a special time for the children in the Chirima household. They would have a long holiday from school, the weather would be at its

48

hottest, punctuated by short, violent rainstorms, and her mother's youngest sister would go to Harare to buy Christmas gifts for all the children.

The family home was a prosperous one. The matriarch of the house was Grace's grandmother, Gogo, and her four daughters and their sixteen children were all housed under this roof. In accordance with Zimbabwean family structure, her mother and her three aunts were all 'Mhamha' - mother - to Grace, and all their children were her brothers and sisters.

Grace's Sekuru, grandfather, had always been a successful man, a government official who had invested here and there in land. He had built a roomy family home near Avondale, a northern low-density suburb of Harare, insisting that he wanted to watch his grandchildren grow up around him. His heart was like a minibus taxi — her Gogo had once said of her husband — there was always room for one more.

The Chirimas were farmers. Gogo was the head of that operation, putting her farm labourers to work daily, digging beds, watering, and weeding. After all the toil, and praying that the crops would not be flooded, or damaged by hail, the time for harvesting would come.

Grace was bright. She loved school and always got excellent results. After she had completed her 'A' levels, her grandfather told her that he intended to send her to England, to study towards a degree. She remembered how happy she had been that day, how open the doors of opportunity had seemed. She had decided she wanted to read English at university, and after being accepted at the University of Westminster, soon the day arrived for her to leave her family behind for three years.

The land of hope and glory had not quite met her expectations. Zimbabwe's colonial past seemed to perpetuate the ghosts of England's past strength and splendour, its civilisation and gallantry. The buildings and parks of Harare and Bulawayo seemed to say patronisingly to their residents, 'Look what fine monuments we English have given you uncivilised people!'

But the people who greeted her in England were so far removed from the British people she had known in Zimbabwe that it was difficult to believe that they were from the same country. They spat, they swore, they were almost impossible to understand. How could it be that a young girl from Zimbabwe could speak better English than the English themselves?

The English winter was also a difficult thing to come to terms with. After lectures she would return to her run-down student accommodation in Harrow and cry herself to sleep, clutching a thin, smelly blanket around her. There was no central heating in the house and she was ill-prepared for the winter. Her winter clothes might have been sufficient for the cold spell in Harare, but they were woefully inadequate here. And her grandfather's food and clothing budget, which she thought was so plentiful and generous in Zimbabwean dollars, would not even cover her food alone.

Grace had never had many friends, and she found it difficult to fit in with the other students.

Never having been without her family before, she was an alien in an unfamiliar world of jokes she could not understand — and the jokes always seemed to be at her expense.

On her fourth morning in the boarding-house, Grace woke up early and entered the bathroom on her floor, eager for a hot shower to warm her bones. Clutching her towel in front of her, she closed the door behind her as she entered, the steam from the last person to use the bathroom still fogging up the tiny space. It only took her a few seconds to notice a foul smell rising up out of the steam.

Grace ran down to the kitchen where she could hear Rachel and Chelsea, the two girls who lived above her on the second floor, talking loudly with their boyfriends. The smell of bacon frying hung in the air and at least two of the group looked decidedly green around the gills. All four looked up as Grace burst in.

"Someone has been sick all over the shower!" Grace exclaimed.

All four burst into peals of hysterical laughter.

"Is someone going to clean it up?" she demanded, horrified.

Chelsea clapped a hand on Grace's shoulder. "If you run the shower, it'll go right down the drain, love. No worries! Gazzer missed the toilet and puked in the bath instead!" She burst into paroxysms of inebriated laughter again, followed by the rest of her friends.

Grace ran to her room and closed the door against the laughter following her up the stairs. She had never felt so angry in her life. Grace Chirima was nobody's maid. She would not clean it up.

She listened to the boisterous voices coming from the kitchen, and heard the front entrance slam shut. They had gone out without cleaning up the mess.

At one point, while cleaning up the vomit from her shower, Grace gagged and almost added to the mess at the bottom of the bath. She tried to breathe in fresh air from the open window and wiped a tear away from the corner of her eye.

A nervous cough interrupted her and she jumped at the sound. Standing in the doorway was Greg, an awkward-looking young man who occupied the other room on her floor. Dark-haired and lanky, Greg's face wore a constant frown, as though trying to ward off unwanted social encounters. Grace had not exchanged a single word with him since moving in. He had not seemed to be a particularly loquacious individual.

"What's wrong?" His tone, although brusque, sounded concerned. Grace told him briefly.

Gently, he took her by the shoulders and marched her out of the bathroom. He made her take off her cleaning gloves and give him the bottle of bleach she was holding. She tried

51

to protest but he closed the bathroom door in her face and she heard the sound of scrubbing coming from beyond it.

Grace had found the first person in England worthy of making into a friend. She was intrigued by his reserved manner and was determined to return the favour.

Almost every evening after supper, Grace would make Greg a cup of tea and knock on his door. He would invite her in and they would chat for half an hour about everything imaginable before she looked up at the clock and declared that it was time for her to go to bed.

Acting on Greg's advice, Grace looked for a part-time job and settled for one as a night cleaner, vacuuming offices by night and attending lectures by day. She would just scrape by.

While Grace was doing well with her studies in her first year, Zimbabwe was not so fortunate towards the end of 2004. The country, having already staggered along the lines of unrest for several years, was showing signs of imminent economic collapse and Grace began to worry for the future of her family.

"I can't sleep, Mhamha," Grace said to her mother on the phone one night in December. "There's so much unrest, anything could happen to any of you guys. I need to come home. I miss you so much." Thinking suddenly of the scenes of violent protest she had seen on the news, she imagined her sister finding herself in the wrong place at the wrong time, or her little nephew going to bed hungry because there was no food on the supermarket shelves. Grace's throat constricted at the thought.

"No, I don't want to hear you talk like this, Grace! Your Sekuru's hopes are on you. You are the only one that had good enough marks to get to England, and now you want to throw it all away in your first year? It would break his heart and you know it. He only has two more years until he can retire, so make sure you give him a wonderful retirement present by getting your degree, ok?"

"Ok, Mhamha, I promise. But I'm still worried about the situation. How is Sekuru going to keep paying for my tuition?"

"Don't worry. Sekuru has put money away for you."

"But what if it gets worse? I don't want you guys to suffer-".

"Where is your faith in God, Grace? Stop worrying and get on with your studies."

As the New Year dawned, the icy grip of winter clenched tighter. Grace thought fondly of the summer she had enjoyed the year before. The parks were so pretty, and everything was so bright and happy. It was like living in two different countries, she reflected, shaking the brown, icy slush off her boots as she stepped inside. Sunrise was approaching and she was thoroughly exhausted. Greg had left a letter for her under her door.

Trying to open it and unbutton her heavy coat simultaneously, she cursed, put the letter down and hung her coat up across two hooks on the back of her door. She opened up her umbrella and placed it in the bathroom to dry, then returned to her room and resumed tearing the envelope open. It was a statement from the university. Over three thousand pounds was still owed for the academic year.

I hope Sekuru will pay this soon, she thought. It should have been paid months ago already. On top of that, Mrs. Hodges, the landlady, had paid her a visit the day before yesterday to ask for January's rent. She had not known what to say.

She had tried to call her mother yesterday, but the mobile phone network was unavailable and the home phone was disconnected.

Grace sat on the floor next to her bed and put her feet in front of a little heater to try to warm up her feet. Her boots had developed large holes in both soles, and every time she went anywhere she had to deal with being in cold, wet socks until she could get home. That's what happens when you can only afford boots from Primark, she thought ruefully.

Just as Grace's mind began to float away in the beautiful lightness of approaching sleep, her mobile rang. She sat upright on the grimy carpet in shock, wondering for a second where she was, then picked up her phone. It was her mother. "Mhoroi, Mhamha," greeted Grace, sleepily.

"Grace, my child. I can't talk for long. I need to tell you something urgently," came Mhamha's distorted voice over the line.

"What is it, Mhamha?"

"Grace, Sekuru is very ill. The situation here is very bad. Inflation is getting worse and worse. Our money is worth nothing!" Grace's mother's voice broke. "We are trying to get Sekuru into Parirenyatwa hospital but they won't accept him without forty litres of water."

"Water? What are you talking about, Mhamha?" Grace blocked her other ear and tried to concentrate on her mother's voice past the distortion on the line.

"Grace, most of Harare has had no water on and off for about five weeks now. It's crazy. Gogo is in such a state. We only get two hours of power a day, too. The shops are empty; we can't get oil, maize, bread, petrol, nothing!" She began to cry.

Feeling the blood drain from her body, Grace did not know what to say. She felt small and selfish for worrying about her financial problems. "What are you going to do?"

"Hameno, Grace, I just don't know. We will have to keep Sekuru here until the council turns the taps on again tomorrow for a few hours, then we should be able to get enough water for him to go to the hospital. But Grace, I needed to talk to you."

One of the girls upstairs chose that particular moment to put some music on at high volume. The sound of Britney Spears came down through the thin floorboards and caused

Grace to run down to the landing on the ground floor in search of a quieter spot to stand.

"Sorry, Mhamha, I can't hear you. Could you speak a little bit louder?" shouted Grace. "What did you say?"

"I said Sekuru may need to stay in hospital for a few days, but after he comes out he might need long-term care at home as well as physiotherapy."

Grace struggled to wrap her mind around the concept of her grandfather's mortality. She was suddenly transported back to a time when she would sit quietly on the porch with Sekuru, trying to get out of doing her chores. If she lay very still on the divan, she could see shapes in the white fluffy clouds dotting the sky and she would tell him what she saw. The porch would be filled with the aroma of her grandfather's pipe smoke and he would harrumph good-naturedly at her fertile imagination and continue to read his newspaper.

"It looks like we will have no option but to use the money Sekuru had put aside for your studies. Ndine urombo, but we have a duty to look after Sekuru."

"But, Mhamha... my rent is overdue and I need to pay for my studies within a month or I won't be able to continue," said Grace, leaning against the wall in the corridor for reassurance. At least that was not crumbling.

"Grace, you are going to have to leave your studies for now and get a full-time job. It would be good if you could send us some money to help. I don't know what will happen if Sekuru can't go back to work. His salary can't even buy food at the moment and I don't know how much longer he will get that money if he can't return to work." After a pause, her voice softened. "Grace, your Sekuru has given us all a good life. Try to see if you can do something to look after him now. Tinashe is leaving for Johannesburg next week to see if he can get work too, so we are depending on both of you."

"I'll try my best to send whatever I can, Mhamha."

"Good girl. I have to go; this phone call is getting expensive. I love you my child."

"Love you too, Mhamha. Bye," replied Grace, removing the phone from her ear and looking at it for some time after her mother hung up.

The train rattled into Finchley Park station, muted somewhat by the noise-absorbing snow falling upon the platform in a bright cascade. Grace darted out of the doors and ran as quickly as she could across the slippery platform and just managed to hop into the Jubilee Line train going towards Stratford. In a rare spot of luck, there were two seats free.

She had been lucky to get this job at John Lewis, she thought. It certainly had come along at the right time, just when she thought she would have no other option but to become one of the people she had so pitied when she first arrived here — the people who slept on park benches out in the snow, or sneaked into the Tube stations at night to keep out of the wind.

God has been good to me, she told herself often, repeating the mantra learned from a young age in a religious household. Yes, indeed. But each night, Grace's mind was awash with regret at the opportunities she had left behind when she dropped out of university to support her family. Her English language professor had begged her not to quit. But Grace could not turn her back on the family. Still, in the dead of the night when she was unable to sleep, Grace questioned everything. Her mother had asked her where her faith in God was, but the truth was, Grace was wondering where God himself was.

Her brother had not been sending money home from Johannesburg. In fact, he had disappeared completely, and after three months the family had no idea whether he had stopped talking to them because he was ashamed he could not contribute, or because something serious had happened to him.

It turned out that Sekuru had suffered a stroke, and he had spent two weeks in hospital, clinging onto life. He returned home after that, paralysed entirely on the right side and needed round-the-clock care. The treatment was expensive and now the state had put him on the pittance they called a disability grant.

Sometimes Grace felt a weight pressing down on her shoulders so heavy that she found it a struggle to breathe. The sole responsibility of looking after a family of twenty was a cumbersome affair, a task that left her feeling dizzy and disoriented at times.

"The next station is Bond Street. Change here for the Central line."

Grace shook herself out of her reverie. Clutching her bag to her emaciated chest, she disembarked. Emerging at the entrance of the station, she began to walk up towards the department store, small flakes of snow dancing around her shoulders like fireflies.

"You hungry, Grace? Here, have some of my supper. I made lasagne," Greg shouted from the corridor. Grace opened her bedroom door, trying not to appear too eager. Greg always seemed to know when she had no money left for food. They went downstairs together and sat in the kitchen, eating in silence. Greg refrained from commenting at the manner in which Grace ran her finger along the sides of the now-empty casserole dish.

"How's everything at John Lewis?" he enquired.

"Oh, you know. Ever since they moved me to the menswear department at the beginning of June, it's been so dull. They cut my hours this week, too. That's why I've been eating your food so much lately," she admitted, feeling the embarrassment burn her ears.

"That's ok, Grace." He smiled at her. "So, do you get a thrill from folding men's underwear, or would you be interested in another job?" he asked casually.

"Another job? Like what?"

"Our receptionist has resigned. So there's a position available, and the pay's all right, I think. Do you want me to put your resume in? I believe you got very good 'O' and 'A' level results."

"Who told you that?" demanded Grace, incredulously.

"You left your resume lying around in the lounge a few months ago. It called out to me. 'Greg! Read me! Read me!'"

Grace laughed heartily. She couldn't help it with Greg around.

Grace hugged herself nervously on the train. She was tired but excited. She hadn't slept the night before, thinking about the approaching interview and her responses to the questions she might be asked. She was dressed in her smart clothes from Zimbabwe, a grey pencil skirt and a neat white blouse. Today would probably be a warm day too, so she hadn't bothered to take a jacket.

July the 7th, 2005. Today was her little sister Tendai's birthday. Yes, this was bound to be a sign of luck.

If she got the job, it would be so much easier for her and her family. She would be able to send more money home, and she would also have enough for food and clothing for herself. Sekuru would be so proud. She looked across at Greg, thinking how much confidence he gave her. He saw her looking across at him and he flashed his warm smile at her.

"Nervous?"

"A little. But how can I go wrong with all the advice you've given me?"

Greg leaned across and took her hand gently. "I know how important this job is for you. I also know you're going to get it, because you're a star."

The train terminated at Baker Street. The next Metropolitan line train to Aldgate was still another twelve minutes away, so they decided to take the Circle line instead.

This train is so slow, thought Grace, frustrated, as she waited for it to arrive at the next station.

"Relax, Grace," said Greg, laughing at her nervousness. "It's still quarter to nine and we've got enough time. See, we're nearly there, it's just Liverpool Street and then we'll be at Aldgate. It's not far to walk from the station. We'll make it, don't worry."

She put her hand in his again, and their eyes met, lingering on each other's faces as though seeing each other for the first time.

The excitement she felt was almost unbearable. That golden door of opportunity, firmly shut and locked for so long, was finally opening up to show her a glimpse of something beautiful inside once more. She barely noticed the doors open and close at Liverpool Street, and paid scant attention to the train pulling away again.

At the very moment the bomb detonated in the carriage, Grace Chirima's heart was filled with one of her sudden, painful longings for home, and the long-unspoken declaration forming on Greg's lips was one of love.

Hajira Amla lives in Johannesburg and has had all kinds of interesting job titles; including musician, journalist, newspaper sub-editor, radio news anchor and PRO. Born in England, she spent two years living in the Seychelles before moving to South Africa in 1993, just in time to witness the birth of a new, democratic South Africa.

Believing that fact is much stranger than fiction, she is convinced that should she ever attempt to publish her autobiography, the Universe as we know it would instantly collapse into a black hole. She has thus decided to delay Armageddon for now, and is willing to accept gifts of chocolate and small furry kittens as tokens of thanks for her kindness.

Lose Myself

Uche Peter Umez

Solid high heels clicked against the hardwood floor, and Chukwudi turned to see a tall, curvy brunette standing before the table that displayed assorted drinks. He watched her, discreetly, as he sipped his drink. He didn't want to admit it, but he thought she looked attractive. Broad shoulders, straight back, plump backside, all emphasised by a trim floral wrap-style dress. He looked away, reminding himself of his vow.

The sitting room was spacious; Chukwudi suspected that half of the furniture had been moved to the basement, to give room for dancing. People lounged in the stairway, sat on the steps, leant against the banister, hovered near the pantry, flitted by the doorway, and sprawled out on some sofas. Everywhere looked like a disco party, without the kaleidoscope of lights. The air pulsed with voices. Cigarette smoke, body odours, and the rounded scents of drinks wafted all around. Chukwudi saw how carefree almost everyone seemed. He thought of his male colleagues who often regarded him as confused and odd, just because he did not want hedonism to rule his life any longer.

'What are you trying to demonstrate? That you're a saint? We're dissolute?' they usually asked. Chukwudi never cared to answer them; they could burn in their excess. He had shocked them even more: every time he went out drinking with them, he sipped only two beers. No matter how much they coaxed and threatened not to hang out with him again. He didn't cave in. They were just a bunch of office workers, so they would never understand what it meant to be a writer, to possess such fine sensibilities, to be able to control your urges, determine your life on your own terms without being influenced by mundane things such as beer and women. In short, how could he advocate a humane society if he continued to live like them; a life of intemperance? Doesn't change begin from within?

Chukwudi sipped his drink. The liquor was smooth, warm, tangy; almost bittersweet. What was the name again, he wondered. Tanqueray? Bacardi? He had sipped three different drinks and couldn't remember their names. The liquor seemed to thaw his worries though, particularly about finishing the first re-write of his poetry collection. His appetite was sharpened as well, though he felt too lazy to get up from his seat. He suddenly realised that he missed his wife's cooking.

Thinking about his wife made him recall the vow he had made to her. A few months after their wedding his wife pleaded with him to always use a condom if he was tempted to sleep with other women. She wasn't going to love him any less even if he messed around, because she knew that 'men would always be men'. She knew his past. He wasn't a womaniser as such, but he had never denied himself any pleasure whenever he happened to find it. But that was before she made that statement; yes, her statement had unsettled him, for it meant that, although he was married to her, she didn't think he was any different from the average skirt-chaser. He couldn't believe that she saw him as someone who was loose and unprincipled, easily taken by lust. Having mulled over that statement, he vowed to prove to her that he could be the faithful husband she wanted him to be. He would rule his passion. She would see that he had changed, that he could make a decision and stick to it.

Chukwudi heard a high-spirited laugh and turned to look. The laugh had come from the brunette sitting on a sofa next to Bayezit, another writer. Chukwudi wondered if the bald-headed Turk was sharing a bawdy joke with the brunette.

"Man, what are you doing here?" asked Cardozo, a Colombian playwright. He sounded high.

"I'm enjoying myself, can't you see?" Chukwudi replied.

"By yourself, man, you're crazy!"

"And you're drunk."

"I'm not, just reeking happy, you Sisyphus. Can't tell drunk from happy, ai?" Cardozo spun around. "Where's the blasted bin?" he asked.

"Check in the kitchen," said Chukwudi.

Cardozo burped. "Huh, man, that's why I lo-o-ve you," he drawled out. "What would I do without you, brother? Why aren't you a girl, ai?" And he tottered off to the kitchen, where a group of girls were puffing on cigarettes.

Chukwudi watched the girls' cigarette smoke form pale corkscrews. He turned as Cardozo lurched out of the kitchen. Cardozo moped around, owlish, and then staggered over to the table, where a bartender smiled at him. Chukwudi noticed the chinos sliding off from his flabby waist and wondered what kind of husband Cardozo would make; a dissipated husband, of course.

"See you around, we're at the terrace," burbled Cardozo.

"Enjoy," Chukwudi replied, almost sneeringly.

Two evenings before, Chukwudi had tutored Cardozo and a couple of other writers that if you were able to quit smoking then no other habit was irresistible. He had experienced the glut, all the sensual fare wanton pleasure could offer. After the heat, what more? He told them how after close of work — before he got married — he would instruct his driver to go and pimp a girl for him. How he ended up having a handful of girlfriends such that he was forced to develop a roster for them, to forestall any friction, or anyone of them turning up unannounced at his doorstep while he was having fun with another girl. Then he mentioned his father, who was even more dissolute than he himself could ever be. A drunk, a complete philanderer. The old man had lived like a pig and was buried as a pauper. No drinks, no music, no fanfare at his funeral, because many of the villagers had regarded him as a disgrace. That was the dénouement of passion. They didn't order more beers that evening. Chukwudi realised his disclosure had soured the mood of his fellow writers. Still he went on, feeling balmy with his speech, a brilliant poet. You get too muddled up when you listened to the stupid crowd. Finally, you expire, miserable; no one would die with his dearest drinking buddy no matter how many cartons of beers they had swigged over the years. He wouldn't waste himself any more, in uninhibited addictions, no matter how much flak he drew from the world. But then he didn't tell them that he had been married for two years and was struggling to keep a vow, which, if he had known at all, he would have made secret; that is, to himself, and not to his wife.

Chukwudi jerked in his seat at the sound of applause. Two girls were clapping their hands while a blonde performed a crazy kind of dance, rolling her hips wildly. Some people hooted, others cheered. Chukwudi noticed the brunette standing in the queue behind two men whose glasses were being refilled. She had a body like an hourglass. She almost spotted him, but he pretended to stare at a portrait above her. Bayezit had moved away, a dark-haired woman had sat in his place. The brunette must be a student, though she looked unlike one. Perhaps, an aspiring writer?

A song started. Chukwudi shut his eyes and lost himself in the lyrics. For a moment, the song hypnotised him. He started wondering if it was really necessary, keeping the vow in such an engaging gathering as this, especially since his wife would never know. He wondered, too, if the international literature conference which had attracted over twenty writers from different countries wasn't some kind of test for him, if the whole thing wasn't a libidinous safari inspired by an unseen Muse. It hadn't been easy for him at all, what with everyone appearing quite friendly and frank, and women smiling too often at him. As one of the discussants he was surprised to note that nearly every writer, aside from him, had peppered his presentation with references to sex as though the whole discourse had focused on sex beyond borders. In his country, writers deliberated more on politics and hunger; not only the hunger of the belly but also the lack of hunger for knowledge among the new generation, youths addicted to YouTube and Facebook. Even drunk writers didn't sound irreverent. But right here, at this international literature conference, Chukwudi felt much more conscious of the degeneration man had plunged into. In fact, his interactions with most of the writers made his mind whip up bleak visions of Sodom and Gomorrah, the collapse of morality.

Chukwudi started when he felt a hand on his shoulder.

"Oops, sorry," said a frizzy-haired girl who had all but stepped on his shoes, but had thrust out a hand in time to steady herself. She wobbled her way to the table.

"Having a good time," Guthoni said; a Kenyan novelist.

"Certainly," Chukwudi replied.

Guthoni raised an eyebrow. "Alone?"

"I'm not complaining, am I?"

"So no catch?"

Chukwudi thought it was a stupid question, so he didn't respond.

"That's the girl falling over you?" asked Guthoni.

"I didn't come here to pick up girls."

"You sound uptight. Hope you're fine, pal?"

"Guthoni, I feel wonderful."

"We're at the back yard, girls rolling over us, as if we're celebs."

Chukwudi stared at him. "I thought you guys were out there on the terrace?"

"Move around, pal," Guthoni said with a wink. "The night is too good to waste away on rumination. After much writing, man needs some mellow flesh." He chuckled and trundled off to the toilet.

Chukwudi scoffed at this and tried to decide between refilling his glass and grabbing some food. He glanced across at the menagerie of meals on the table, and saw the brunette loading her plate. His stomach rumbled. He stood up and walked over to the table. The brunette slid away to the next meal, as though avoiding contact. He scanned the table, unable to decide at once what to eat. He reached for a plate, and she exclaimed: "Sushi."

Chukwudi turned, thinking she had spoken to him. But she had only expressed her delight, he noticed. She picked up a sushi container and dipped a finger into it. He saw the tattoo on her neck — a dragon coughing out fire.

"Nice," he said.

"Yes," the brunette said. "You want to try it?" She gestured to the sushi. He followed the direction of her hand. She lifted a small roll topped with shreds of fish and what looked like coloured rice and handed it to him.

Chukwudi said, "Thanks. I actually meant your tattoo."

The brunette touched her neck. "Oh. Thank you."

Chukwudi wondered how he was going to eat it.

She noticed his confusion, said, "Let me show you." She squirted some sushi into her mouth. "You see?"

Chukwudi squirted the sushi into his mouth, too.

"You like it?"

He made a face.

She smiled. "Try another one?"

"OK," Chukwudi replied.

"It goes well with ginger slices or the soy sauce over there," the brunette explained, pointing at a bowl of coppery-looking liquid and a small plate covered with the pink strips of what she called pickled ginger. She took half a teaspoonful, sprinkled it on two sushi rolls and gave him one. "You'd love it."

Chukwudi chewed, warily. "This is good."

She moved the plate to her left hand and offered him her right hand. "I'm Selena."

Somehow, he felt ticklish as the softness of her palm caressed his.

Selena looked expectant. Chukwudi knew she expected him to disclose his name, but he thought it was useless introducing himself because she would never remember his name after tonight.

"I'm from New York," she added. "You're from Africa?"

"I'm from Nigeria," Chukwudi said. It irked him whenever people presumed he was African simply because he was black. Did it occur to her that he could have been from Jamaica? Brazil? Surinam? Even America?

His seat was occupied, he noticed, when he turned round. A man and a woman absorbed in conversation.

"Seats all taken." Selena read his mind.

Chukwudi shrugged.

"There's space upstairs."

"Upstairs?" He raised an eyebrow.

"Another sitting room," Selena said.

The sitting room seemed more spacious than the one downstairs. The walls gleamed with bright wallpapers. Four sofas were laid out in different corners to form mini booths. Doors faced each other in a corridor that led right down another stairway. Couples sat in two of the sofas while a lone smoker, a Chinese-looking man, lay on the sofa blowing smoke into the air. Chukwudi and Selena picked out a padded green bench facing a polished desk with an antique typewriter and an old chessboard on it. Just above the bench loomed a large portrait framed in glass and oak. The portrait caught his fancy. It showed a profile view of two faceless people trying to touch their fingers together, but for some reason distance separated them. Chukwudi grinned as he thought about the girl standing next to him. They would never get close, he thought, because of his vow. He and the girl could as well be the faceless pair.

"What's that?" Selena asked.

"Don't mind me," Chukwudi replied, wondering how she would react if he divulged his thoughts to her. Would she take it politely? Or think him odd, too?

"Please tell me."

Chukwudi almost told her, but then said, "I visualise a lot."

"That's cool," she said. Then, with her fingers, she combed her long hair. "What do you make of the painting?"

"Umm…" He racked his brain for an idea. "Forget it."

Selena seemed disappointed. "You're one of the writers for the conference?"

"I don't exactly see myself as a writer."

"Pardon my ignorance; what does that mean?"

Chukwudi sat down. "I'm more of a poet."

Selena sat down next to him. "What's the difference?"

"Anybody can be a writer," he explained. "You too could be a writer. Get a journal and collect your thoughts. Then send it to a publisher, and…" He raised his hands "…and, well, poetry is a different thing. Quite profound."

Selena looked confused now, though she asked, "What would you like?"

Chukwudi noticed how the words had flowed mellifluously out of her mouth. He tried not to look at her round pink lips, which he found inviting. He looked away, chiding himself inwardly. Yet his mind couldn't help but flash an image of those evenings he used to enjoy himself with scores of girls, after having swilled five or more bottles of Gulder.

"Do you want something to drink?"

"Oh." Chukwudi shelved the image out of his mind.

"I want Absolut. Okay, with you?"

"That would be fine."

Selena smiled. "Okay."

As soon as she skipped down the stairs, Chukwudi thought she was fun to be with, someone you could talk with for hours, without feeling bored. Or tense.

Selena reappeared with two small glasses. "Here you are." She handed Chukwudi a glass. She brought some strawberries and green grapes in a small plate. He wondered what she wanted to do with the fruits. "Vodka and whisky are the same, do you know?" she said, tossing her hair over her shoulders.

"Vodka is Russian?" asked Chukwudi.

"Yes."

"And whisky?"

"It's the Scots. Whisky is Celtic word for water of life."

Interesting connotation, Chukwudi thought, as he sipped his drink; it tasted both hot and cold on his tongue. "My knowledge of liquor is somewhat limited."

"We all have our share of ignorance." Selena sipped her drink too.

Chukwudi started to feel too conscious of himself, as if he was afraid that he might give in to an illicit feeling he thought he had long reined in. A part of him wanted the party mood to leach into him, another part raised walls to ward it off. He didn't want to get carried away by the frivolities around him, yet he found it hard to simply relax and enjoy some banter with the brunette. Nothing could go wrong, he assured himself. He was in control.

"Have some." Selena broke the silence.

Chukwudi gazed at the plate, thinking of Eve in Eden. But unlike Adam it wasn't an apple he was being offered, just strawberries.

"Try it with the strawberry, it enriches the flavour," Selena said, pointing at the fruits, already chewing one.

Chukwudi noticed her fingernails were unpolished as he picked a strawberry and put it in his mouth slowly, as though he feared he was about to chew something piquant. Slower still, he chewed. His face crinkled in a sudden smile. "Are you a connoisseur or what?" he asked, smiling.

"I like exploring," said Selena.

Me too, he all but blurted out but he checked himself in time. Chukwudi then thought of asking her if strawberries came in different varieties. Like apples. Earlier in the day, the sun blazing over the blue sky, all the writers had been chauffeured to Wilson's Orchard. Chukwudi had been amazed to find out that there were so many different varieties of apples. Why was he thinking of apples now?

"Good," he said, nodding vigorously, as if to dismiss the question from his head.

Selena offered him some grapes. He picked two out of her palm and tossed them into his mouth. She raised her glass and swirled the drink with her finger. Then she swept her tongue over her wet finger, licking it.

Chukwudi shuddered as a picture of his wife licking his nipple rammed into his mind. He clenched his jaw in annoyance. What was wrong with him? Why was he acting like a horny fifteen-year-old? How could he not hold himself after just a few drinks when he was used to gulping down half a carton of Gulder? But that was more than two years ago. No, it wasn't the drinks! It was the atmosphere, he thought; it was too… affecting. And it didn't help that everyone was carrying on in a who-cares-about-the-next-day manner. But almost all the writers had been like that since they arrived at the conference, hadn't they? So that could not explain why he was feeling so whimsical. Chukwudi didn't want to admit it right away, but he couldn't well deny it altogether: the conference had spanned two weeks already and he had never stayed away from home this long. As funny as it might sound, the longest he had stayed was five days. Even most of the conferences he had attended in Nigeria hadn't lasted more than three days, and they often fell on weekends.

Gazing into Selena's brown eyes Chukwudi was reminded of home. And yet he had a fortnight to stay in Illinois. He longed for his wife, truly; he missed her so terribly that he couldn't help seeing flashes of her in Selena's every gesture. Perhaps, he shouldn't have accepted the drink. Perhaps he should have kept to himself and avoided this brunette.

"Do you have a timepiece?" He hoped the van would be picking them up soon, though it was due shortly before midnight.

"I don't like carrying one around," Selena said.

"Why?"

"Makes me too mindful of things I haven't done yet."

Suddenly, Chukwudi didn't feel comfortable sitting so close to her, although he liked the fact that Selena wasn't wearing any make-up, or earrings. He respected girls who made up lightly or didn't put on any at all. It showed self-confidence in a girl.

"Are you OK?" Selena asked, twirling some strands of her hair around her forefingers.

"Just tired." He yawned.

"I am sorry. You... must find me boring."

'No, no; it is the atmosphere."

Selena stared at him. "Stifling, yeah? And cold?"

Chukwudi dropped the glass on the table next to the typewriter. "Do you mind if I ask you a personal question?"

"How personal?" she asked.

Chukwudi pointed at her tattoo. He had always found the motifs and the motives behind each individual tattoo fascinating. He didn't think he would ever wear one, yet he wasn't pleased with the way Westerners abused it. Tattooing was an ancient art, a visual kind of poetry, revered and numinous. The more people regard it as a fad, the faster it lost its mystery.

"Dragon, you like it?"

"Cool." Chukwudi pictured her as someone with a fiery temper. Why else would she choose a dragon and not a butterfly, a flower, something more feminine?

"You know about dragons in your country?" Selena asked.

Chukwudi gave her a baffled stare. What kind of a question was that? Didn't she know dragons were fabled beasts? Was his country antediluvian? "What informed your question?" he asked.

"Dragon is a mythical creature."

"It's obvious!" he snapped.

Selena looked stung. She seemed not to have expected such an outburst. She apologised and finished off her drink.

Chukwudi gulped his drink down. The liquor singed his throat. "I don't know what got into me."

"I didn't mean to offend you…" Selena started to say.

"Forget it," he cut her short, quietly scolding himself for sounding curt. "I overreacted."

"I only wanted to explain how we view dragon in the west," Selena spoke very fast as if afraid he might snap at her again. "It's very different from the way the Asians see it. The Chinese believed dragons are a symbol of gentility. Here, we regard dragons as deadly creatures."

Chukwudi forced a smile. "Tell me a little about yourself."

Selena smiled back. "What do you wanna know?"

"Things you feel comfortable talking about."

Selena got up abruptly. "I got to pee, excuse me."

She darted off, knocked on a door, went through it. She seemed to know her way around the house. Maybe she was a regular here; every time the occupants hosted a party for the international writers she would show up. She came out shortly after, and sat down so close to him their hips touched. She started rubbing her forearms, like someone who was cold. The air was chilly and smelled of pine and eucalyptus. Everybody had sneaked away except the lone smoker, now snoring on the sofa and a brownish-skinned girl sprawled out on the other sofa. Chukwudi noticed the large window behind the girl's sofa. Outside, an oak tree waved its raspy leaves lightly. Amid the rustling wind, crickets chirped. When Chukwudi turned his head, Selena was holding out a hand to him.

"Let's explore," she whispered.

"Huh?" Chukwudi said.

"I can't stand the chill, let's find somewhere warm."

He wanted to follow her, but hesitated because he didn't think it was wise to stay all alone with her in an isolated place. "I think we should go downstairs."

"I want a place we can relax without feeling frozen." Selena giggled. "You're scared?"

"Don't be ridiculous," Chukwudi said.

"Come on, then."

Chukwudi's stomach tightened as he took hold of her hand. He felt tempted. Selena pulled him along like a boy. She paused at the first door, rapped gently. A gruffly voice replied, "Buzz off! Room's taken."

Selena winked. "He's busy."

She knocked on another door then waited for a response. She rapped again, but nobody responded. His stomach constricted some more; his throat was parched. He wondered what she was up to, even though he suspected her of leading him on. Suddenly, he snatched his hand from her grip and said, "I think we should just go."

Selena swung round to face him. Her breath, tinged with soy sauce and garlic, filled his nostrils. "Go where?" she asked, almost reproachfully.

He looked at her lips, and clenched his fists. "Downstairs."

"Nobody is inside this room. Let's just check. Okay?"

"Are you crazy?"

"You're afraid."

Chukwudi scowled, but Selena ignored him and twisted the door knob. Bright orange light swamped both of them. She poked him in the ribs. "Voila!"

The first thing Chukwudi noticed was the ornate bed, its thick eiderdown marked with floral patterns and large green pillows. The bed looked like it had never been slept on. As he turned to tell her they should leave now since her curiosity had been satisfied, the door slammed shut and he was squashed up against it. Selena plastered her mouth over his, her tongue sweeping the dry corners of his mouth. Chukwudi tried to break free, but she strung her leg around his calf, while the other leg pinned him to the door. Her breasts crushed his chest, and he couldn't breathe well. She clasped his hand over her buttocks, and flames exploded along his spine.

"No, stop it!" He pushed her away with his might. She tried to reach for his hands, but he pulled away. She swung round and leant her back against the door, blocking his exit.

"I can't do this." Chukwudi panted, feeling his penis harden.

"Why not?" Selena asked, with a frown. "You think I'm a pro?"

"No," he stuttered.

"What's wrong? You're gay?"

"No, I'm not."

"I'm not attractive enough for you?"

Chukwudi found her desirable, but he was at odds with himself. He wanted to lose himself in the moment, since no one would know about his escapade. Yet, at the same time, he longed to steel himself against temptation, uphold his two-year-old vow. "It's just that..." He trailed off. He couldn't tell her about the vow, his quest to remain faithful to his wife. She would probably laugh at it and regarded him as naive. "What if someone walks in on us?" he asked.

Selena held his eyes as she sashayed up to him. "Nobody will," she whispered. "Trust me."

Chukwudi realised that it was likely he wasn't the first writer she might have cornered in a room. Was it an amusement for her? A game of sorts? He stiffened as she started with his buttons. His hands shook when he tried to peel her fingers off from his shirt. But the first button had come undone already. She stroked his nipple, and his buttocks tingled. "Why are you doing this to me?" he whispered, looking over to the window, wishing he could steel himself against the crush of desire.

"I'm so cold." Her voice was thick as syrup.

He gripped her hands. "This is crazy. Stop..."

Selena chewed on his lips. Then, suddenly, her dress slid off her body. Chukwudi turned quivery as he saw how devastating she was naked. She wasn't wearing a whiff of bra or panties. Her flesh stood out ripe and cerise like the apple he had munched at the Orchard. His mind blurred as she tossed herself into his arms. They both staggered on to the bed. As she tried to pull off his shirt, he slapped her hands away and yanked the shirt off and flung it to the floor. He couldn't think of anything now except that she had set him alight and he could regain his senses only when he was burnt to a crisp.

Selena leant over him and reached for his zipper.

"Wait," Chukwudi whispered, as he noticed some stickiness between his legs. He wished he had a condom. In his passion, he had ejaculated prematurely. He managed to smile at her while kicking off his trousers to the floor, but then the door creaked open. Both of them threw the bed sheets over their bodies as a couple stumbled into the room.

Chukwudi went limp at once as Guthoni regarded him with a scandalised look, then with an amused grin. He was a chatterbox, and would spread the news about Chukwudi in a minute, not to hurt him though, just for the mere sake of fun. Guthoni slung his arm over his partner's shoulders, a small African-American girl with an afro, and they lurched out of the room. Before the couple finally shut the door, he heard Guthoni chuckle and say, "Carry on, doggy dog!"

Chukwudi could not look Selena in the face. Silent and sweaty, he crawled out of the bed and eased into his clothes. Selena called him back as he reached for the doorknob. Maybe to apologise, maybe to pick up where they had left off, but he didn't want to find out. He didn't want to stay in the room any longer. He had all but broken his vow, so he was no longer sure he could trust himself not to give in to her advances a second time. He didn't want to think about the vow any more, not now, not here, for it seemed his wife had judged him correctly. Men would always be men? A surge of anger passed through him as those words flickered through his head. And he pushed the door open before she could reach him. Chukwudi didn't look back as he bounded down the stairs and strode out of the building.

Stuffing his hands into his pockets, he glanced around the cold dusky night, hoping to spot a cab, while trying not to let in the image of his wife, curled up under the blanket, awaiting his return from America. Guilt twisted through his heart, and Chukwudi felt he would never be able to make love to his wife again, without the brunette's face hanging over his head like a sword.

Uche Peter Umez is a poet, short fiction writer, and a children's novelist. An Alumnus of the International Writing Program (IWP), USA, he has participated in residencies in Ghana, India, and Switzerland and won a few awards for his writing. He has been a Highly Commended winner twice in the Commonwealth Short Story Competition, 2006 and 2008 respectively. His short stories, poems, reviews and non-fiction have been widely published online and in print. Uche lives in Owerri with his wife and their children.

Uncle Jeffrey

Murenga Joseph Chikowero

Willie fingered the small packet in his side pocket. He had opened it several times these past three days to look over the small blue tablets inside, but each time he had suppressed the urge to throw two of those blue things down his throat. Perhaps this Viagra business was really meant for old white men who live in cold places, and could really damage a tropical African like him in the long run? And what if he became one of those users who ended up with a stubborn erection that lasted for more than 24 hours? An erection was the very thing he dearly wanted but who wanted a permanent erection, especially over this Christmas holiday at his parents' rural home? And what in God's good name was keeping his doctor from making that call?

It was already three days from the day he took the test and two days before Christmas Day and still no word from Dr. Khan. Could it be that the man had gone to India? He never mentioned India and in fact made a big deal about being an indigenous Zimbabwean — an Indo-Zim as he called himself — one of the few local Indians Willie knew who spoke Shona at every opportunity. Willie sometimes felt the young doctor tried too hard to belong, but still found him likeable enough. What could have held up him so? Willie wondered again, as he made for the grass-woven bathing house a distance from the homestead.

Sure enough his mother had set out a pail of warm water, even though this was clearly going to be one of those boiling December days; when heat-waves shimmered just above the ground, and mirages of clear water appeared in the blazing distance.

Willie's wife, Tatenda, had dutifully placed the sweet-smelling bath soap, bath salts, and aftershave gels, on the washstand. As if to confound her mother-in-law, Tatenda had also placed her own bigger pail — of cold water. Willie smiled as he undressed. The undeclared war between the two women was still alive although it had long ceased to be a pitched battle; both now seemed to resort to guerrilla manoeuvres. But, small guerrilla tactics were almost welcome compared to the raging quarrels that had characterised the first five years of his marriage to Tatenda when Mai Willie, as everyone called his mother, had insisted she would never have a muKorekore — a funny-talking Northerner — for a daughter-in-law. A cleverly-plotted trip to Karoi, Tatenda's home area, two years ago with Mai Willie had eased the tension a bit.

On that trip, Tatenda had surprisingly been on her best behaviour. The headdress, and zambia wrap had never left Tatenda's body throughout the three-day stay in Karoi. In fact, Willie gently teased Tatenda about her new-found traditional ways, and he asked if this was the end of the activist who usually saw the hand of patriarchal domination even in women's traditional dressing styles. Willie still remembered Tatenda's gentle response that night under the cool bed sheets in Karoi: "I need to experience oppression in the flesh to know how best to fight it".

Willie stretched to his full two metres and cast a few glances over the grass wall in the direction of the kitchen. Tatenda, his two sisters, and Mai Willie, must be preparing the afternoon meal in there. These days they shared recipes and laughter as they went about it, though they still seemed to be trying to outdo each other in subtle ways. Satisfied that no one was coming, Willie took off his shirt and neatly folded it before placing it on the makeshift shelf. Before removing his grey Bundu shorts, Willie tapped the side pockets to satisfy himself that his cellphone was there. On second thought, he unzipped the pocket and took out the slim gadget. He cursed himself for letting Chido, his favourite sister, use up all his airtime. Even Mai Willie's rather long conversation with Tapuwa — Willie's older sister who worked in England — was not really necessary.

Now Dr. Khan wasn't phoning and he had no way of contacting him.

Stark naked, Willie hesitated before looking at himself. Though he had tried every trick to avoid sleeping with Tatenda in the three months leading to Christmas, his member was limp and thin as a piece of biltong. His mind went back to that day in Woza Woza Hotel when, in a frenzy of soccer celebration, he had bedded a prostitute, the first and only time he had betrayed Tatenda.

He still didn't know what exactly sparked the riot in the bar, but from the hotel room upstairs, Willie heard the sharp police siren piercing the late Friday night air. It wouldn't do for him to be arrested and then fined for consorting with a lady of the night, or to be part of a riot at a seedy brothel that masqueraded as a hotel. Sprinting out of the room, Willie had guessed that the back stairs might not be guarded yet. After stepping off the last rung onto a jagged broken bottle in the dark hotel backyard, he remembered that he had forgotten his suede shoes in the room upstairs and that he had not paid for services rendered. Or more precisely, services half-rendered. Still, nothing could be worse than having his drunken face in the daily papers. He had removed the sock and covered the smarting foot, before limping off towards his car.

He had praised himself for at least remembering to use a condom, in addition to seeing his old friend Dr. Khan for an HIV test the following morning. A few days later, he posed what he thought sounded like a sufficiently hypothetical question to a lowly but reportedly wise workmate at Datanet Research Services where he was a senior statistician: "If you were doing research on this muti business, would you find anything solid that is really used to fix unfaithful men?" Muzivi, the elderly cleaner — whom younger university-educated colleagues like Willie still called 'Teaboy' behind his back — had laughed long and loud at this. He stopped briefly only to start another loud and unending howl before snorting a few nuggets of snuff. Shaking his spare body almost imperceptibly, Muzivi sneezed once, twice, and then nodded before winking at a bewildered Willie. Rather theatrically, Muzivi then walked over to the sink and properly washed his hands as he was required to do by company health regulations, before coming back to stand near Willie who was still trying to make everything appear very casual to the three girls at the reception. It was only the second time that Willie had ever stopped to chat with the older man.

"If you did the thing with one of these women of the night and ran away without paying then boss you are finished. And especially if they steal something like a belt or your shoes," Muzivi said with a straight face.

"No, not me, just curio-," Willie started.

"No need to lie. You are not the first to ask, boss. Thank God she isn't married otherwise you might have been on central locking system right now."

"Central locking system?"

"Yes, boss, same as in your car. Stuck together right at the loins," Muzivi said, now curiously displaying no emotion whatsoever. "Or she could have used her magic to take your organ," he added.

"To take my..."

"Sure, boss. The whole apparatus so that the whole place would look as smooth as ruware," Muzivi said with a wink, referring to the smooth rock pavements dotted across the country.

It was at that point that Willie decided against telling Muzivi that he had in fact been avoiding his wife because he had lost his potency after the brothel incident. Dr. Khan expressed shock at the risks Willie was posing to Tatenda through his reckless behaviour, and for a second he thought he felt his testicles retreat into his stomach. In his righteous anger, Khan had needlessly spoken against any sexual activity until two HIV and STD tests had been done, the second of which would be done at the end of the viral window period. The first test results eased Willie's worries a bit, but Khan had shaken his balding head and insisted that the first test could mean nothing at all.

"Come back for another test after three months," he had said.

"What! I have a wife. What will she say?" Willie asked. He was horrified by the prospect of confronting Tatenda with the news that they would have to be celibate for the next three months for reasons which, well, he couldn't quite reveal.

Tatenda had thrown a tantrum after he came up with one excuse after another. He had quickly enrolled for a Practitioner's Advanced Diploma in Statistics with the Open University. He installed a large reading desk in one corner of the lounge and piled thick books on it and pretended to read well into the young hours of the morning. When he resorted to switching off his cellphone and going straight to Manhede Sports Bar after work, Tatenda had stormed out and briefly moved in with a female friend.

But in the end, he had survived the torrid two-and-a-half months and had taken the second HIV test a day before they drove home for Christmas. Khan had rubbed his shining forehead and promised to call him when the results came back from the lab in a day or two. However, sexual potency seemed to have deserted him forever, at age 30, just when Tatenda had started talking about replenishing the Earth with a brood of Willies. After all she was a year older than him, and Mai Willie was becoming restless on that front too. Only two days ago, Mai Willie had made vague references to some village girl who, according to her, came from 'a good family'. Still, Willie had persuaded Khan to prescribe him some aphrodisiac pills, which he had not had the courage to take in the absence of the results from the lab. He carried the packet on his person at all times and made a point of lying on it when he sneaked into bed.

He was almost driving out of their homestead when his wife emerged from the kitchen.

"Where are you going?"

"To see Sekuru Jeffrey."

"Oh, I always enjoy Sekuru Jefu's company. I just have to join you," she said, tying and retying her zambia and edging towards the front passenger door.

"But Tatenda... you are cooking aren't you?"

"Yes, but Mai Willie will happily finish preparing my soup. And Tete Chido is now a big girl as well."

"What do you find so attractive in that lazy loafer anyway? He keeps refusing to come to Harare, but I heard his pig of a wife gave birth again two months ago."

Tatenda cooed gently. She stuck her head inside the car and said, "That means he has five children now. Sekuru Jefu must know something that some men don't. OK, let me go ask Tete Chido to keep an eye on my soup, before I tell you exactly what Sekuru Jefu and I are planning to do tonight while a certain man makes love to books," she said before tapping his cheek and turning back towards the kitchen, swinging her waist suggestively.

"Is that walking or dancing?" Willie asked her retreating backside.

As soon as Sekuru Jeffrey recognised the blue car leading up the footpath to his home, he walked out of the kitchen and observed the slow-moving vehicle with keen interest. Even before the car eased under the lone muhacha tree, he leapt into the air and landed on one knee, ceremonial axe already stuck in his armpit, palms beating a steady rhythm as he intoned:

"Eh! We salute you Shava
The Bull Eland
Impregnable fortress
Beautiful smooth walker
We salute you Mutekedza
You who was given wives in the land of the Njanja

We have seen your good works Great Bull..."

It embarrassed and yet fascinated Willie to see the older man do this. Arms stretched out, he dashed towards his mother's brother who stood up to reveal trousers with holes at the knees and a coat whose sleeves reminded Willie of merciless storms and helpless banana leaves. Still, he let his dusty uncle hold him close and celebrate his annual homecoming.

Tatenda was already organising two of Sekuru Jeffrey's younger daughters to carry groceries from the trunk into the small, smoky kitchen. Sekuru Jeffrey's own wife, the strangely rotund Mbuya MaDhuve, at last emerged from the kitchen, stuffing a large breast into her battered top, and ululated while uttering praises in a high-pitched voice before skipping like a girl to embrace Tatenda who stood there smiling. In the end they all trooped into the kitchen where Christmas goodies were quickly shared to more ululation, more praises, and brief prayers to both God and the Ancestors who were keeping watch over the descendant of Mutekedza, who continued to plunder the fortress of Harare to bring his people all these nice things. No reference was made to the ancestors of Tatenda even though she had actually bought most of the goodies from her own earnings, but she didn't seem to mind at all. As soon as Mbuya MaDhuve got down to asking Tatenda if she wanted her bones to start creaking before starting to have children, Willie winked at Sekuru Jeffrey who obliged with a brief nod. The two men clapped their hands as they walked out of the house — backs half-bent although the door was large enough to allow even taller men to walk past comfortably.

Back under the muhacha tree, Sekuru Jeffrey quickly found a wet mop and started dusting the blue car as Willie briefly sat on one of two stools and leaned against the ancient tree.

Willie stood up and inched towards the older man. "You don't have to worry, Sekuru. The dust can't do any harm," he started. It was an old argument which he never won, but one he felt had to be made.

"No, a prince must always show his true colours," Sekuru Jeffrey protested.

When his uncle had finished his business, Willie opened the driver's door, slid in a CD, the one that had Sekuru Jeffrey's favourite song, "Shauri Yako". Willie understood a little Swahili but had heard enough local singers trying their own versions of the song to know its wide appeal.

"This takes me back to Mgagao in Tanzania, my nephew," Uncle Jeffrey said. He had fought in the liberation war and had been trained in East Africa.

From the glove compartment he pulled out a Marlboro cigarette carton. He extended it to the older man who pulled on his own home-made cigarette at one end of his mouth, while one hand accepted and held the shiny Marlboro carton at an angle as if admiring its very newness.

With much deliberation, Sekuru Jeffrey gave the carton back to his nephew. "Open it," he said. "But why should I open this for you, Sekuru? You know I don't smoke," Willie protested.

"I just wanted to confirm that I won't be sharing it with you," Sekuru Jeffrey said with much laughter.

It was another old game they played every Christmas holiday, but it never ceased to make both of them laugh with the special satisfaction of two boys comparing the size of their penises. Willie held out a long, thin cigarette and Sekuru Jeffery lit it using the butt of his home-made one. Willie then handed back the whole carton and said with a nod towards the kitchen where keen, feminine voices could be heard, "Your niece wants a baby."

"So you want me to have two wives? I can't speak English to her," Sekuru Jeffrey said in mock helplessness.

Willie didn't laugh. "I had a problem three months ago and things have been difficult since. I am avoiding her." The older man merely eyed him. "The Big Eland has gone to sleep," Willie added quickly although his uncle had already understood the nature of the problem.

Sekuru Jeffery closed one eye and pulled at his shiny new cigarette, kept the smoke in his mouth for a while before expelling it in three neat plumes above his head.

"I don't have a disease or anything like that but I just, you know..." Willie said in what he later recognised to be a whisper.

Sekuru Jeffrey pulled again and repeated his ritual, this time expelling the smoke from the left side of his mouth with a quiet satisfaction. When he saw that the cigarette was half-smoked, Willie opened the trunk of the car and brought out a large bottle of whisky. Even before he sat down, Sekuru Jeffrey called out to one of his children to bring two cups. The older man turned the bottle over a few times, admiring the inscriptions and images that told of places whose exotic mysteries only his tongue would taste. He then handed it back to Willie who uncorked it with exaggerated difficulty. He poured for the older man and again enjoyed the little ritual argument over why he still didn't drink whisky when he had no problem drinking lagers. Sekuru Jeffrey took a long pull and let a few drops run down his impressive beard and onto the lapels of his jacket.

Willie sat and listened to the older man talk about his youngest girl who was showing much promise in first grade, about his crops which might still do well if the rains fell soon, in fact, everything but the issue Willie had raised. Only after the third cupful did Sekuru Jeffrey disappear into his thatch bedroom to emerge with a dubious packet that he handed over to his nephew.

"Take just once. Sprinkle a thumb-pinch into your relish. Please fill me another cup," he said in virtually the same breath.

Willie tried to appear casual as he went into the kitchen to bid the women farewell. They all came out and embraced Tatenda all over again. Willie was taking precise instructions from Sekuru Jeffrey about exactly how to negotiate the meandering drive to the main road. He made a great show of listening even though it was the same route they had used just two hours earlier.

"I struck a deal to be Sekuru Jefu's second wife," Tatenda teased. "Mbuya MaDhuve has no problem with that as long as I keep supplying them with sweet urban things." She eyed him for a reaction before adding, almost as an afterthought. "And in case your friend Khan hasn't told you himself, the results were negative. I took his call late last night. You had put the phone on vibrate so I gently frisked you when I kept hearing the brr sound."

The announcement hit Willie so violently the car swerved before somehow steadying itself. His tongue stuck to his palate.

A few minutes later, Willie looked across at his wife who was humming along to Ilanga's *True Love*, the year's hit song and noticed her smooth round thighs just under the thin zambia, then her dark brown face. It was, above all else, her smooth dark complexion that had made him beg to carry her books from the university library to her apartment eight years ago. A gigantic snake stirred in his stomach and coiled downwards. The feeling was so urgent it made him drunk. They had not yet reached the main road and to each side, a shoulder-high maize crop waved in the lazy afternoon sun. Willie turned his head all the way back and noticed the family behind him had gone back into the kitchen to enjoy their Christmas goodies. He parked the car under a muzeze tree, killed the engine and went round to Tatenda's door. She was already reaching out when he opened it and together they ran into the maize crop to the right, half-bent at the waist. A strange light shone in Tatenda's eyes as she laid out her zambia, while Willie folded his T-shirt into a kind of pillow and placed it at one end.

Twenty minutes later, Willie led Tatenda back to the car, hand in hand. A thin figure hovered near the car and made false throat-clearing sounds.

"I wanted to make sure the car is safe." With that, Sekuru Jeffrey lit one of his new Marlboro cigarettes and pulled contentedly as he walked towards his home. Bluish plumes of smoke spiralled lazily behind him. At the end of the bend, he shouted loud enough for the two to hear, "Madhuve tells me you are taking one of my girls to Harare. See you when the holiday is over."

Murenga Joseph Chikowero was born in Mhondoro-Ngezi, Zimbabwe, at the height of the 1970s liberation war. He was raised there, learning to fight other herd-boys and listening to the legends of the Manhize Hills. He studied English-language literature at the University of Zimbabwe before teaching at the Zimbabwe Open University. In 2010, he worked with Peter Orner and Annie Holmes on an oral history project which gave birth to the highly-rated book, *Hope Deferred: Narratives from Zimbabwe*. He has published short fiction in *StoryTime* and in the anthology, *Where to Now? Short Stories from Zimbabwe* (2010). He enjoys reading and writing about history and memory in Southern Africa. He is a doctoral candidate in African Literature and Film at the University of Wisconsin-Madison.

The Times

Dango Mkandawire

Imagine if you will, the terror that would ensue if a dark and thunderous cloud slowly descended upon an unsuspecting crowd, and within this misty blur, one could sense the sparks of a thunderbolt forming. Now consider yourself standing helplessly within this mob unable to determine either where the tail of the bolt would appear or the direction of its bellowing arrowhead strike. Once a week, such was the apprehension in Blantyre, Lilongwe, and Mzuzu, the three major cities of Malawi, and if we are to believe Thucydides' report that the strong do what they can and the weak suffer what they must, then we can say that the strong had moved, doing what they could, and as always, they were confident to secure their place.

"I don't think you understand what I have been saying to you," said an ambassador of the strong who had introduced himself as Gordons Phiri.

"I understand perfectly," Richard Chirwa responded.

Like two bulls with horns locked in firm grip with razor sharp eyes and shuffling hooves to maintain balance, they engage one another in dialogue, each manoeuvring words to gain the advantage. Richard Chirwa is seated at his desk, his elbows on the surface and his hands clasped together. Gordons, a stalwart figure with a heaving chest, is standing opposite, having been courteously offered a seat that he rudely declined.

"You don't know what you are dealing with!" Gordons continues, donning a suit-jacket that is a size too big, incongruent with his body shape and size, the sleeves covering his palms so that fingers suddenly dart out from the fabric when his arms are relaxed, giving him the appearance of a man who approximates towards style, appreciating the finer things, but not quite able to own them as they were intended to be owned. A dubious-looking Versace tag is still attached to the sleeve.

"I have listened intently and, as far as I can see, it is you who doesn't understand," Richard replies, not breaking his gaze even for a moment from the open newspaper gawping at them from the shiny desk. "I don't discriminate. I gauge every story on its merits and if we, as an editorial team, decide to print it, you might as well put on your reading glasses."

Silence.

Gordons sizes Richard up, partly surprised but mostly amused at the courage he is displaying for someone whose appearance is so accommodating and unimposing. An elfin man, round-faced and beady-eyed, Richard carries the demeanour of one who has lived his whole life avoiding confrontation, slipping past people without friction. A man with no skid marks to his personality. Gordons wonders whether Richard's confidence is based on a truly strong will or rather stems from wishful ignorance, grounded in the mistaken belief that no actual harm could come his way — the counterfeit courage of many. He finally sits down.

"You see, Richard..." Gordons has previously called him Mr. Chirwa, but now he adopts a more lax tone. He reaches into his inner jacket pocket and pulls out a gin sachet, slicing it open with his incisors and downing the contents, steel-faced without wincing. "People like you don't need to be in situations where you have to meet people like me. Just looking at you I can see you're a decent man. Didn't you go to Kamuzu Academy? The Eton of Africa they called it, whatever that means! You think because of that you are better than me!"

"Yes, I did go there, but never at any point-".

"I never went to school," Gordons interrupts. "Or rather, I did for a while, but I have no piece of paper-certificate, diploma, whatever! that can confirm this. We both know being uneducated in a Third World country means poverty. A dollar a day, I have heard. But yet..." This time he reaches into his trouser pocket and pulls out a brandy sachet, and once again his face is impassive to the sting of corrosive liquor. "Yet I drive a Mercedes-Benz. How do you think I manage this, to make my living?"

Gordons leans back with his hand to his chin and it's as though the air around him has suddenly thickened and for the first time since this man stormed in unannounced, against the rebuke of his secretary, Richard is genuinely nervous.

"This summer has been the hottest I can remember for a long time. Maybe you need to think about this overnight, when it's cooler; to come to your senses, to ask around." Gordons reaches into his pocket and pulls out a pair of white-rimmed sunglasses and moves as if to make his exit, but stops at the door. "Throughout my life, what has always amazed me is that it's those who have never been in actual fights, never had a broken nose, who speak most heroically of violence, of making a stand and all that. Those of us who know better tread carefully. For we know why men fear. It is obvious that there is no reason for a man the stature of Leston Barrassa to appear in your little paper. Do the right thing." He puts on his sunglasses and walks out.

Richard sits with the same taut posture he has maintained throughout the discussion, staring at the portrait above the door through which the thug has just left — a picture of his only son. He sighs deeply.

So it begins, he thinks. Threat number one. Protect your old man, Junior. Me, you, and Thomas Nast will not budge. He picks up the newspaper, packs it into his drawer and locks the office, three hours early.

So this is fear.

"It's all this western influence, I tell you! It's destroying us," says George Patterson, the General Manager of Malawi Water Board, engulfing the telephone receiver with his plump hands, the sweat of his podgy cheeks moistening it.

Beston Banda, the Malawi Water Board Operations Manager, on the other end, listens silently as George perfects a tirade in slander on western influence. "I agree," he responds, pretending to sound concerned.

"Everything is being westernised. Look at this Madonna nonsense!"

Beston smiles to himself as he recalls the image of David Banda that had been displayed on television before and after the music star Madonna had taken him away from the land of his birth. He was no longer the same boy. Had he remained, his life may very well have been but a gamble between the four horsemen of the apocalypse casting lots to see who would claim him. The specifics of international law aside, Beston is happy that the child was adopted but, once again, his tongue is programmed to agree on default with everything George says. "It is nonsense."

George continues to denigrate everything from what he considers to be Madonna's ill-conceived adoption of an African child to rap music. Caught in the rhapsody of his own monologue, George reaches a grand crescendo to his complaint. "Who is he, this Richard Chirwa?" he says. "And what right does he have? This shit is sold on the street in full view of everyone! Children seeing their fathers, mothers, uncles, and aunts, disgraced. This is un-African! He deserves to be shot at point blank range!"

Beston feels execution would be rather harsh, but he will not rally to the defence of the editor to rescue him from this brash criticism. The only saviour he knows is called Christ and he inherits the earth. Within these walls, 'merit' is merely understood to be a rarely heard word such as 'uxorious', a word whose meaning one may know, but no tangible benefit can be realised from knowledge of such a term. A good word to know is 'sycophant' for, in this company, it is the sycophant who inherits the promotion. Let the best man win.

"Indeed," he responds, startling himself at the quickness with which he replies.

It is only now that Beston's attention is fully engaged and considering what could be the source of such a scathing attack, he wonders... could George be next? It is Thursday evening, just hours before distribution and maybe someone within the publishing industry has tipped him off?

George hangs up and Beston gladly returns his attention to the newspaper on his desk. Initially he had ignored it, regarding such a publication as befitting unemployed gossips and the like; fodder for women in salons as they fried their scalps in the name of beauty. However one day, quite ashamedly, he pulled out his wallet and bought it... Emblazoned in bright red font, the headline screamed: PASTOR WAS TOLD TO SUCK ON CHOIR LEADER'S PRIVATE PARTS!

"What do you mean it's your child?" Simon asks with a tremulous voice.

Having been in boarding school for a year, he gazes upon her now plump face before looking down at the baby lying motionless in its crib. "You're a virgin. We're virgins." At eighteen years old, having just finished his high school examinations, and awaiting university selection, Simon imagines either he has not heard correctly or a second virgin birth — he genuinely considers the latter.

Janet, upset, stands at arm's length away from him, but not quite distraught. "I am sorry," she says, trying to placate him. "I really am."

He had arrived there with flowers and chocolates, awkwardly carrying these delicate gifts in the rusty, decrepit minibuses Ndirande is notorious for. The men ridiculed him for his gentleness, while the women cheered him for his sensitivity, and the journey became a grand battle of the sexes.

"Now, here is a shining example for you men to follow," said one woman gripped by nostalgia, remembering when, long ago, she had been at the receiving end of such pleasantries. A curious eulogy began on the untimely death of romance, contemporary men being deemed vulgar and crass, unlearned in the arts of wooing.

The men fought back, retaliating, counter arguing over how women of this age were not worthy of receiving such chivalry.

"Men simply do what they must to get a woman into bed! If we needed to be polite, we would do that. But it isn't necessary because you have set the tone!" An enthusiastic gladiator of the Empire of Man valiantly declared to the roar of the mobile coliseum.

However, in the midst of this exchange, when Simon indicated to the driver where he needed to be dropped off, one of the men broke out triumphantly in elated laughter before subsiding."You bring flowers and gifts to girls who live here?" he said with a crumpled face.

The women, who moments ago had been his vociferous admirers, now recoiled into a subdued silence, amnesia erasing their previous excitement and adulation. Simon hadn't cared. It didn't matter to him if Janet was not rich. Neither was he, though his family fared better than hers. He was relieved when he finally disembarked, not because he felt shy — nothing in the world could make him feel uneasy about her — but throughout the journey the door on his left seemed to be unhinged and the conductor was keeping it in place with his arm and thick rope. This is Ndirande.

"I can help you raise it," Simon says. "I don't mind. I forgive you."

She looks down, shaking her head, before telling him she is in love with the baby's father. The word 'love' disorientates him.

"I don't want you to ever call me again or come here," is the last thing she says to him. Despite his effort not to, he starts crying, silently, with sobs inwardly reaching out to her. His tears remind her why she left him. He was still a boy and she wanted a man.

The baby's old nanny — her face overwhelmed by perplexing wrinkles, not from old age but testament of a life of struggle — sits at the other end of the room, fixing her gaze on them. She cannot speak English but, just by observation alone, she can hear everything. Flowers? Chocolates? How nice. But wholly unnecessary. She thinks to herself. Simon is unaware that he is in a prostitute haven.

Simon walks outside, and as he does so, he now understands who the father of the child is. He gives the man a quick pitiful glance, seething with a pathetic and helpless rage — pointless even — unable to do anything. He has been broken, devastated by the world, and he submits to the flames engulfing him from all directions with licks of sulphur. He has been so drawn into his encounter with Janet that he hadn't even let go of the flowers, clutching the stem of the roses so tightly the thorns are digging into his palms, making them bleed. Before turning away, he takes one last look at the scene before him. Janet's man is seated in the warm, comfortable leather of a GX Toyota Land Cruiser, number plate WATERBOARD 9.

Friday morning. The offices at Malawi Waterboard are rustling like leaves with excitement. The 137 members of staff have three designated messengers who go around the offices distributing the newspapers. On a normal day, employees pool money together and one newspaper is shared by at least eight people. On Friday, however, one newspaper is shared only by three as most want their own copy so that they can read it with greater freedom in the confines of their homes. Upstairs, George is seated in his spacious office staring into space with a Kasparovic glance as he waits for fate's opening gambit. He isn't going to do any work today. The only reason he has shown up is to minimise the inevitable ridicule. He can hear them already, "That fool even ditched work to try and avoid embarrassment." He will not give them total satisfaction. He will take it like a man.

George has heard from whispers in the street that his name is on the front page. He tried all he could to change this outcome, but all the usual means of persuasion failed him as though *The Weekend Times* was being sold in stone tablet form, its letters engraved beyond edit. He vividly remembers the last conversation he had with Richard Chirwa.

"Richard, wouldn't you like a nice holiday package with your wife and children at the Sunbird Nkopola Lodge during the Christmas season?" he asked him.

"A wife I have, but children I have none," Richard replied after some silence. "Anyway, I am far too busy this year for a holiday."

George Patterson had even asked him in Chichewa. George hardly ever speaks it. Since he was a boy he has noticed that many mixed-race people in Malawi don't converse in it. They only do so when they have to. Since his adolescence he has considered it barbaric and, though he has all the inflections and accent, he deliberately speaks it as though he were a tourist fumbling through the words. With Richard, however, he spoke perfectly.

"Pitani! Mukasangalale!" He says, telling him to remember to enjoy himself.

There is a pregnant silence before a response.

"We are men who believe in some sort of justice. How would it be fair to the pastor of the large evangelical church, who was the main attraction of last week's edition? Following circulation, he lost half his flock as they splintered due to the newspapers' expose on his hypocritical lifestyle. With the pastor, we had to consider the social impact of having a major religious figure being disgraced, but we still printed. People with God as their employers could not effect a moratorium of our activities. What would stop us from printing your story?"

With that, Richard hung up the phone, and George was left with the receiver glued to his cheeks. He couldn't believe he had been rejected so quickly... and with such wit! That was on Wednesday, two days ago.

From that moment he braces himself and prepares for the worst, and on this cursed Friday he wonders if God wouldn't save Pastor Nkwande, what hope do sinners such as he, have? George looks at his kangaroo leather wallet by his desk and immediately thinks about his money. This scandal may very well be what tips the scales and Angela will leave him. Whatever they have left, whatever anyone can call it, it is a mockery of a marriage. He can already see her, immaculately dressed as she always is, shaking her head as she reads the paper before tossing it violently into the bin. Divorce is on the horizon. With melancholy, George lets his mind freely wander to a time when women would rather be bruised and battered within a marriage than step out of their houses — or, rather, legally speaking, their husbands' houses — as divorcees. Times are changing.

"It's all this western influence," George mutters to himself.

Richard Chirwa had once been a jovial man. The kind of person who saw a potential friend in everyone he met. He laughed frequently. However, unknown to him, a cosmic hand had shifted the predictable path of the stars onto an uncharted route. The fear of every couple with a single child materialised into a nightmare when their only son Joseph died. As the gravediggers shovelled thick layers of dirt upon the coffin, the Earth's crust mercilessly engulfing Joseph beneath his feet, Richard heard with his right ear the clanging sound of a chain breaking forever. Immortality lost! He had no heir. Along with his son, he bore the unbearable pain of burying all the hope a father can have for his own humble contribution to the world, for the future. Richard was breathless as he experienced the monstrous perversion of having to bury his own child. Joseph had died of the scourge, AIDS.

Richard became a different man after this. Eating little, saying even less. What haunted him most was one conversation that he'd had with Joseph when he fell ill, after he had told his parents his status.

With vacuous pupils he suddenly began to speak. "Father, it was Brenda. I got it from her. I am sure of it."

"Who is Brenda?"

"Brenda Malikebu. She was my girlfriend." This was the first time in his life Joseph had ever told his father that he had a girlfriend. "I trusted her totally, even though I was told that she was a little wayward in her dealings with men. I didn't listen! Love, madness, whatever it was... I would've given two years of my life just to touch her shoulders," he burst out, sobbing while his father nodded with the understanding of the elders; sympathising with the frailty of the young. "I had been faithful. I had loved her. I am afraid I can never forgive her for the life she has stolen from me, but I fear that if I die without forgiving her..." He coughed violently, squeezing the sheets with his hands. "I will end up in hell... I must forgive!"

Joseph wept bitterly that night. Reservations about his father's presence aside, it was the most intimate hour in both their lives. Richard had stood sturdy, monolithic in strength during this time for both Joseph and Joseph's mother, Annie. Many things were shared between the three of them, until the day Joseph died. And what a young man he was. Twenty two years old.

The number seven is different to the number nine. That difference could be two units, or something impossible to quantify. In this case, when an adolescent by the name of Simon was asked to write down his story, somewhere within his narration he wrote down a number plate for a vehicle. The only problem was Simon's nines tend to look like sevens. When he flicks his pen to sketch a nine, the little circle tends to be too thin and protruded and the leg is straight rather than curved. His teachers had always told him this and he had lost marks in some of his maths classes as a result. In this instance, the difference between a seven and a nine was WATERBOARD 9: George Patterson, General Manager and WATERBOARD 7: Beston Banda, Operations Manager. The latter a happily married man, the former a frequent adulterer on the brink of divorce and flirting with its greedy sisters, alimony and settlement.

Beston is holding the newspaper in his hand, blinking rapidly. His arm is stiff, motionless, as he scrutinises the print. The peculiar looks he received earlier now make sense. Sheila, his wife, didn't pick up any of his calls previously. Knowing her, she must be hysterical by now. Or maybe not. This situation has no precedent. He cannot predict how she might react. He storms out of the office amidst the half-hidden glances of satisfaction from the staff. He ascends the steps into the General Manager's office where he finds George drinking a coke. He holds the newspaper up before he says anything, pointing at the headline.

"I have to leave the office for a while, George. I have to sort this rubbish out."

George feigns surprise, having been one of the first people in the country to get a copy, imagining how ridiculous he must look with raised eyebrows.

"Beston, Beston, Beston. You too? I told you this newspaper was no good."

Beston retorts that he didn't do anything, but George just shakes his head and reminds him that he had better go and 'correct' the situation. As Beston walks out George stares at the open door. He has decided to deny everything to the point of obscenity. Absolutely everything! And he will use Beston as the scapegoat. How far it will get him he cannot imagine, but it's his only lifeline.

Richard had been working for many years at *The Daily Chronicle* and had reached a point where he began to wonder why he got up in the morning and drove to work. A man's writing is his mirror and portrait. Every time he wrote something that was later edited so extensively that he could not see himself in the script any longer, he would transpose himself back into the lecture halls of the Malawi Institute of Journalism and recall the words of Mr. Hastings Sangala, his lecturer: "Every journalist has only his credibility and his reputation to rely on." He would hear the words echoing every time he read a paragraph that was no longer his, but had his name on the heading. He was an opponent of this media corruption only in his mind, the years passing without him ever protesting, though he wished he had the mettle to do so. He endured the drudgery, having struggled with monotony, but finally accepting that the best part of his life was past, and realising that the routine of later life is just as natural a part as the spontaneity and idealism of youth.

Then Joseph died.

As he quietly drifted through the wilderness of mourning to find meaning, standing at the precipice of inner death, a curious sequence of events resuscitated his heartbeat. And it all started with pornography.

Pornography in all forms is illegal in Malawi. However, 'unsavoury' pictures of a very prominent citizen had been leaked onto the internet. The poor man — being of another generation ignorant of hidden files and passwords on a personal computer — had sent his laptop for repairs and forgotten to delete his more than prurient photos. If only it had fallen into the nail polished hands of a woman, just maybe things would have turned out differently. But, alas, it just happened that his laptop was between the fingers of a young man of twenty-seven years with all the passions of that age.

From experience, the young man discovered that any personal computer that comes in for repair that is owned by a man will most likely have pornography of some sort stored somewhere. He always knew how to look and, once again, his hypothesis proved true. With the generosity of a philanthropist —after a decent attempt of blackmail that wasn't taken seriously, being seen instead as a bluff— he shared the pictures with his friends and they did likewise until, in a matter of days, they littered the digital highway. The man in question stood askance when the young man sent him a complimentary DVD for refusing to offer bribes. Soon, the unsung entrepreneurs of Africa, raggedly clothed, had burned DVD copies and were selling them in the streets. Richard himself had received an email with some of the material and had ignored it. But not for long.

His attention wasn't drawn by the less than nubile bodies that were on display, but rather the reaction to the images. One man, an avowed dinosaur who had vehemently refused to learn to use a computer in a solo attempt to preserve the age of letters, suddenly approached Richard requesting him to teach him how to use the internet for 'research'. He kept pestering Richard, who saw through his intentions and asked him directly.

"Would you like to see the sex photos of the Minister of Agriculture? I have them. I can print them for you."

The fossil shook his head in disgust and walked away, wishing, Richard suspected, he was not so outwardly prim and could have just said yes.

As the days passed, he noticed huddles of people gathering around computers like rugby scrums, jeering at what they saw. It was everyone. Cleaning staff who had heard and had asked their superiors if they could have a look, junior management, senior management... everyone. The family was mortified, embarrassed beyond description. One of the minister's children had to be withdrawn from school, face splashed with tears, because of the teasing.

What surprised Richard were the number of stories about the Minister of Agriculture that sprang up and the names that were mentioned just as a result of this incident.

Richard listened with greater and greater irritation at the details of this infringement of privacy, and decided to sit in the cafeteria by himself. Having nothing to do, he picked up a copy of the newspaper he had found at the table, even though he had already read all the important bits. He was now just rummaging to pass time.

He happened to stumble on the 'Did you know?' column, which is one of those random columns that speak of some arbitrary person or fact. For example, did you know that Coca-Cola would be green if colouring weren't added to it? That sort of thing. On that day, however, was a caricature of a curious man by the name of Thomas Nast. He was seated holding a long pencil, long as in javelin length, sharpening it at the tip with a knife. Not far from where this Nast fellow sat was a hefty man with a plump belly and a moneybag for a head. It turned out, generations ago in the United States, Nast had been a cartoonist and the hefty man, Boss Tweed, a man in government, swindling millions. Tweed was so terrified of Nast he tried almost everything to stop him from publishing drawings of him that depicted his corrupt practices. Eventually, his downfall was partly attributed to Nast and his ruthless drawings. Richard thought about this the whole day, wondering how ludicrous and ridiculous it was for a grown man to cower before the artistic shades of a cartoon...

The days lingered and the town still talked of the Minister, now thoroughly a laughing stock. Richard then thought of the role of shame. If the Samurai would go so far as to disembowel themselves, or members of one's family would commit honour killings to abate shame, to atone for it, could he use it, this very same shame, with tinges of embarrassment, to make some sort of difference?

It was as though time folded as a great expansive sheet and he was in the same space as Thomas Nast, a man in another age who also, with limited means, used his abilities to fissure the crust and strike the core, he with a pencil in drawings, Richard with words in sentences. From this was born *The Weekend Times*. His subjects wouldn't be movie stars and musicians like in the West. They would be business men, managers, CEO's, the kind of people in the exclusive minority who can send several children at once to European universities. Everyone knows who they are.

He would be relentless. He would include their phone numbers, their addresses, the names of their mistresses, the colour of their briefs — everything. The thunderbolt hovered above anyone who was high enough to dare scrape the silhouette of cumulonimbus clouds. It wouldn't stop here. He would also sweep the earth for those who were masters in anthills, rulers in their own small enclave who had developed a reputation.

The Weekend Times is the only newspaper printed in every major language spoken within Malawi, and in a deliberate manoeuvre to amplify anticipation it is released into circulation only at noon on Fridays. And the whole country waits. From school children counting their coins at the newsstands, looking for the fathers and mothers of peers to provide fuel for teasing, to nervous, egotistical politicians and the general public, itching for a story, all holding their breath. Like Hugh Hefner who, in 1953, had monetised the hidden lust of America with Playboy, so Richard Chirwa monetised the gossip of Malawi with *The Weekend Times*; an alchemist changing hearsay and rumour into printed ink and giving the masses the opium they had learned to crave. He became the capitalist face of Malawi's scandal. And in just two years it made him a rich man.

Dzone Country Club was a shrine where entrance depended on an almost obscene membership fee. Its colourful members were no different to the whites of the colonial era in the sense that they were all devoted to making it what it was — an ultra-exclusive oasis.

Richard had spotted a young man coming out of the doors and on closer inspection had determined he was picking up his inebriated father and it made sense. To be here means you have arrived in the world, and to have arrived in the world your hair would have greyed, that silver in your beard becoming a hard currency. This is not a land where an industrious twenty-six- year-old African Steve Jobs can collect his apples in a basket, take them to market and become one of the wealthiest men in the country... even after taking a bite in every single one of them. Seniority matters.

With his new-found wealth, Richard walks in for the first time and, as soon as his shoes brush the mat, the voices around him hush and thin out, the sounds of a woman stirring her gin and tonic suddenly amplified. He ignores the uneasy attention lavishly bestowed on him; instead, he spots Leonard, a friend of his, sitting at the bar.

"Hello Richard," Leonard greets him uneasily, hesitant. They talk, Leonard taking the lead, his topics superficial, every word carefully crafted; a mere theatre prop to disguise what he really wants to say until another glass of whiskey frees his tongue, springing it from the back of his taut throat.

"Why are you doing this?" he hisses, and leans in closer to Richard to stress his point. "Look at everyone. We were all having a good time until you walked in. I know someone who rushed to the back entrance almost knocking the waiter over for fear of featuring on the front page of your newspaper. Men will be men. Come on. You cannot tell me you haven't had an affair in your life. Hypocrite! Where is this puritanical nonsense coming from? If we want preachers we will get them in church." He whispers through clenched teeth.

"It's got nothing to do with church or sin or marital faithfulness," replies Richard. "It's about life and death. Responsibility! More people have died of AIDS than genocide. We were better off dodging blood-dripping machetes in Rwanda during '94 than we are now in 2010. With our small urban population, this place is an explosive cesspool unless we do something. For goodness sake man, we have seen entire families wiped out before our very eyes. We need to change our behaviour!"

"Change our behaviour? Change-our-behaviour," he stresses, almost jumping up. "You really believe that racist nonse-".

He stops and raises his eyes above Richard's head. A woman walks into the room with the self-assured confidence that can only be spawned from a lifetime of flatteries.

She wears a bright red flowing dress, almost a cliché in a badly-written book. Everything about her is beautiful — her skin, eyes, her presence. She stirs Richard from his hidden depths as she walks past all of them to the other end of the room where she sits down, her movement gracious as though choreographed in advance.

"Who is that young lady?" Richard quizzes.

"Do not even look in that direction," replies Leonard. "That's one of Leston Barrassa's mistresses, Brenda Malikebu."

"Brenda Malikebu you say…"

"Yes. They say she is the most stunning. And there are many." He sips his whiskey before placing a cautious palm on Richard's shoulder. "I received word that you had plans of printing a story on him. How stupid that would have been."

Richard doesn't respond, the face of the sachet-drinking thug in white rimmed sunglasses, who had warned him that those who make a stand may break their noses, flashing momentarily before his eyes. He drops his eyebrows, unable to understand what he is feeling. He looks again at her, beautiful from every angle and in everyway, her fingers well-proportioned and shaped, nails ebony black long and captivating, as she delicately grasps a glass of wine. No wonder Joseph had loved her.

Leonard, sitting next to him and witnessing this transitory trance, mistakes it for lust and lets him have his moment of indulgence before breaking the spell. "You need to feature yourself in your paper! Look at your wayward eyes!"

Richard ignores this.

Leston Barrassa walks into the room.

His cauldron of a belly lavishly arches outwards, his mouth as wide and loud as always, reminding everyone of who he is and what he has. He takes his place next to the beauty, fitting in comfortably.

Richard had perceived it before; it had been talked about on radio and television, and LoveLife had erected billboards in the city depicting it. For the first time, Richard had finally seen it with all its screeching halts, skid marks, and wreckages. He was standing at the side of the sexual highway they had been talking about for all these years and had seen a headlong collision. And in the burning wreckage and fumes was the limp and smouldering body of his son. The others would follow eventually.

Richard quietly slipped out of the building before things became incomprehensible.

That night, as he stared upon the soft brow of Annie as she slept peacefully, he remembered how they were when they were young; when unbridled youth was their lot, excitedly searching for a companion. It was so different! He felt a deep sorrow, not only for his late son Joseph, but for an entire generation of young men and women. Men born in an age that didn't buffer for mistakes, not even those inherent with youth. Men, who could put their lives at risk for loving a beautiful woman — a woman who the powerful would also desire. Women, who could give up the ghost for falling for a warrior, a man of charm, a man of influence. And yet, all this is natural. And could this generation, could this same-seed basket with calves suffocated by skinny jeans, transcend itself — just so it could live... Do they even know what 'transcend' means?

Richard sits with his elbows on his desk. It is 13:15. He knows that the newspaper has been distributed and, by now, the arrows of gossip may have pierced Achilles' heel. But this isn't mythology, a world in the sky, in people's heads. This is the world of cement and brick and, in this world the arrow may have done nothing more than cause an irritating scratch.

He can hear a commotion from downstairs, chairs falling, shouting, a man saying something about how he is a manager and will sue for libel and defamation, but Richard does not bother to find out what is happening on the first floor. He has bolstered security at the premises and now waits to see the day finish, with him the passive observer, body limp, slouched in his chair.

Leston Barrassa is on the front page, rumoured to be the richest man in Malawi, whose ventures range from legitimate business, to grey areas, to blatant criminality. A man no one wants to get on the wrong side of. A man with a small standing army of thugs on his payroll.

Many decisions have been made to get to this point. He has also decided to get tested. This time for real. Straight after work.

Richard looks at the copy in front of him almost in disbelief, as though he himself had not written and published it. Premature ejaculation. His wife having an affair with a member of his household, his kitchen staff to be precise — an act of revenge apparently. A brother rumoured to be a homosexual who had taken on an expatriate lover from Germany. He stops reading the article four times to take breaks to recover. So much detail. Normally he leaves his team to come up with the stories and he reviews them but this time he did all the work himself. Never before has he delved so deep into the private life of anyone. But he feels he had to do it. To do all that one is able to do is to be a man. To do all that one would want to do is to be a god. He is a man.

He is Thomas Nast reincarnated.

Dango Mkandawire says of himself, "I write because it is in literature that we are able to see ourselves; the letters' mystical mirrors, divine prisms angled in all directions so that we see all our parts — so that we reflect. I write for it is discovery, and count it a great honour. I currently live and work in Blantyre, Malawi and spend the bulk of my days in a blur of bewilderment at the unexpectedness of life that is understood when one awakens the senses and is able to see beyond the routine and realise there is no boredom in existence."

Snakes Will Follow You

Emmanuel Sigauke

I had been lying on a reed mat, reading *Julius Caesar* in the shade of our tsapi — the hut on stilts I used as my bedroom. As soon as Brutus stabbed Caesar, I looked away from the page to avoid picturing the sight of blood. That's when I saw it, a baby snake slithering towards me. At first, I thought my eyes were tricking me, so I closed and reopened them, but there it was, calmly drawing closer and closer to the mat. I jumped and screamed, but covered my mouth as soon as I remembered I was a man. I glanced in the direction of the kitchen hut to check if Maiguru, my elder brother's wife, had heard me; then I stiffened and watched the advancing snake.

When it reached the edge of the mat, it coiled into a neat, little wheel and waited. My heart beat faster, but I knew it wasn't because of the snake; no, it didn't scare me at all. Ignoring my heartbeat and the beads of sweat on my forehead, I leaned forward to examine the snake. Its shiny, black skin was decorated with white spots. I had never seen anything like it before, a snake with tiny green eyes that looked at me with seeming recognition. Its head peeked out of the coil, and, although I didn't know how to read emotions of snakes, its face looked relaxed, like how we relax sometimes in the company of friends. For a moment I considered the possibility of making it my new pet, but quickly remembered that danger often disguised itself as innocence and beauty. Maybe it was not alone; its mother or father might have been waiting in the grass on the edge of the compound, planning to attack as soon as I had been hypnotised by its baby. Yes, that's what this was: a trap.

I stood up, tiptoed backwards, my eyes still focused on the danger. If this was a warning of more dangerous things to come, I didn't want to discover the truth too late like the fallen Caesar. If anything, I had to show that it was I who was more dangerous than the snake. Fear was out of the question here; this was just a baby snake, so, truly speaking, I was just moving back to get a better view, to observe a curious creature's behaviour.

The snake must have noticed that I was trying to escape, for it uncoiled and slid towards me again. This wasn't good. Why couldn't it leave me alone? I back pedalled again, but my escape ended abruptly when my back bumped against the wall. The snake stopped, but then resumed, flowing along the edge of the mat. I wanted to shout something, to call Maiguru, but my mouth refused to open, and I felt my eyes widen. This thing was still advancing, and for a moment I thought it had started to transform, to grow bigger. For some reason I began to think that it was using its magic, perhaps to confuse me. I closed my eyes again hoping it would vanish, but when I reopened them, there it was, still small, still slithering, slower, as if it had all day to pursue me.

What did it think it was doing? I didn't have time for games. No room for fear. I stiffened again, for the third time, and looked directly in its eyes. However, its eyes seemed not to see mine, as if it was now blind. I could feel my body shaking, but I didn't want to show that I was afraid, yet the longer I stared at its eyes, the more scared I became. I couldn't afford to show fear. I had to be the more dangerous beast, I, Fati Shumba of the lion totem, the courageous one. King of the... But the snake was still sliding forward unhindered by my silent totem pronouncements. It started moving faster and was getting closer and closer to my bare feet.

I snatched my book and hurled it at the snake. At first I thought I had missed, but saw the book covered the whole body except the tail, which wriggled briefly and went limp. I frowned. Just the fact that my book had come in contact with the serpent, or the possibility of its pages stained with juices and innards, disgusted me. Saliva filled my mouth and I spat; then I tiptoed closer. Before I girded myself to touch the book, I rubbed my hands together. Even my hair bristled, and a new surge of courage seized me. I checked for movement — of the book, or of the tail — but there was none. I smiled and pushed the book aside with my big toe and jumped back, only to realise that my toe hadn't even come in contact with the book. Still, I wasn't afraid — this little snake was nothing to fear. I crouched and pinched the book by its spine and lifted it. The snake's head had been flattened and the tongue sticking out lifelessly. It even had a tongue! I felt a new wave excitement build up, and I was now ready for more snakes; let a whole nest of them come. I checked one more time, just to make sure it was dead. It didn't stir.

This was the perfect time to call Maiguru, who was in the kitchen hut cooking. She came out running and sweating. I could tell she was confused by the urgency, or excitement, in my voice, and that although she was walking towards me, towards us, she could easily go back into the kitchen if she decided I was wasting her time. You could see it in her eyes, which were full of questions, blinking rapidly. I beckoned her with rapid jerks of my arm. She advanced with her sideways, eyes-down look she always gave me when she thought I was acting silly; but I knew that soon pride would spread all over her face, and she would finally know that, despite my brother's absence, there was still a strong man in the house.

"What happened?" she asked. "I thought I heard you scream but remembered that-".

"Watch out!" I cried. She was going to step on the snake.

She stopped, looked on the ground and stumbled backwards. After she regained balance she said, "A-ah, why would this surprise you?"

"And you're not surprised? Scared?" I asked, pointing at the dead snake.

She shook her head slowly and said, "The prophet told you already. Were you listening?" She waited for me to respond, but my mind was already on the prophet.

I suddenly remembered what the prophet had said only a week ago. I was surprised that I had forgotten about it in the first place. It must be the studying that occupied my mind. I looked at the lifeless snake for a moment, then at Maiguru. "And you took him seriously?" I asked, realising though that I too had taken him seriously. I had no choice but to take prophets seriously; that was the only way I could make sense of my life at the time. But, I had not expected the spectre of the snakes to start this soon. I had somehow believed that it would not happen for a while.

Maiguru stood there acting normal like the snake was a small matter. She even looked at it like she was the one who had killed it. She looked at it like one appreciating a piece of art.

"I'm surprised you don't look scared," I said. "At least you should-".

She raised her hand to silence me. Then looking away from the snake, she said, "He was clear with you." She looked back at the snake and pointed at it with her toe. "Until you leave the village, this is what will happen." She coughed. "Every week, every day, even every hour, whether you like it or not."

I didn't like that—how she said *whether you like it or not*; I didn't like it when all my choices were taken away from me. "But this is nothing," I said. "It's just a baby. Look at it."

She didn't look directly at it; instead, her eyes traced its trail and stopped at the edge of the compound where the grass began; then she turned back to me and said, "Did it try to follow you? Did you try to run?"

"I don't run from baby snakes," I said, pumping up my shoulders. "You know I don't run from anything."

She gave a brief laugh, much like a cough. "This is not a test of your manhood. A prophet says something, you listen to that prophet. Hear?"

I shook my head. Listening to prophets was one thing, running away from small creatures was another. Big difference there. The thought made me grin, to confuse her. But she looked too serious to be confused. She clasped her hands and started chewing her lips like she was ready to solve a puzzle. This time she was looking at the snake directly. I looked at it too, more daringly. There was always something reassuring in the ponderous Maiguru, but I didn't want her to be a muchekadzafa in this situation, no point in her trying to solve a problem I had already solved.

The bald prophet had said snakes would follow me, or 'do funny business', to put it in his words, but how was I supposed to know that they would try to disturb my studies like this? I was just a student who didn't bother anybody. What did they — the witches, the snakes, even the prophets or whatever — want from me who had nothing to offer except a bunch of borrowed books? But that was the problem: I had too many books and, in the eyes of my enemies, I might actually succeed in life. The prophet had said the witches didn't want me to amount to anything.

Maiguru bent to take a closer look at the snake. She looked fearless, nodding the way she did when she thought only she understood what was going on. "Yes, this is the kind that would follow you around, the innocent kind that witches will send."

"Yeah? And you know this how?"

"My ears, unlike those of someone I know, were open when the prophet talked. And I think this is just a warning. This is them being nice."

"Them who?"

"You know who I'm talking about. Who else would send snakes?" Her face darkened, like something was biting her insides. "Do you even care about all this? About your safety?" She was breathing heavily now. "If the witches succeed in their plans, even these little books you are reading will all go to waste. Corpses don't write exams."

Most likely, she was right; I just didn't want to hear more of this now, but then a funny thought seized me, something connected to what I had just read. "So it's saying watch out for what may happen in April?" I said, stopping short of adding, something similar to the Ides of March? But with Maiguru, it would be a waste of time. She wouldn't get it. She didn't have a clue about literature, and sometimes I thought she was better off not knowing these things. I felt guilty even thinking about her in this way. Therefore, I rephrased my question, "So this is a big warning, as if something major will follow?"

She didn't answer; in fact, she stood in a domineering, plan-hatching posture which dwarfed my sense of importance. It was as if I hadn't said a thing. I felt better.

We stood there, she examining the snake, making plans for it like she was the one who had killed it, I trying to draw closer but ending up moving back. Not out of fear, but to allow some breathing space between us.

"Does this have anything to with this being April 15?" I asked, feeling naughty again.

"Something like this could happen any month, any week, any day," she said, straightening and fixing her skirt, which had started crawling up her thighs — which for some reason I was beginning to notice, often feeling guilty for noticing. Maybe the skirt was already hitched that high when she bolted out of the hut. She always fixed her skirt that way when she cooked, as if she wanted the light brown shade of her thighs that contrasted with the darker legs to peek at the world...

She straightened and frowned. I looked away. "It could be any hour, any minute," she said. "Just be careful."

I nodded and picked up my book, looked for sticky stains on the pages and started wiping random pages on my shirt, but I stopped when Maiguru raised her hand.

"What happened?" I said.

"No, you don't do that!" she said.

"Do what?" I said, looking to see if my free hand was doing something it shouldn't be doing.

"Don't be the first to touch that book." She dashed forward, her hand extended. "Give it to me, let me be the first one to touch it. If they choose to follow and harm me, that's better. You're still in school."

"But I have already touched the book," I said, coughing out a laugh.

"Just pretend you didn't and let me be the one to touch it first, on purpose," she said, extending her shaking hand.

There was no way I would let her take my book. I needed to resume my studying.

Didn't she realise that I wasn't afraid of snakes, nor the witches that sent them? I had an English Literature test on *Julius Caesar* the next day, and this was not the time to worry about what there would always be time to worry about. I clutched my book closer to my chest and stiffened for the fourth time since the arrival of the snake.

When she saw that I would not relent, Maiguru dropped her hands and shook her head the way my elder brother, Mukoma, did when I had not completed a task the way he wanted; a gesture that was always a prelude to a sound beating meant to correct my ways, or as the villagers liked to say, a good panel-beating. I resented Maiguru for shaking her head like that. Who did she think she was? Certainly not my brother.

I leaned against the wall behind me and started flipping through the pages of my book, although my eyes kept looking up at her, to see if there was something wrong with her. She seemed not to notice my presence anymore, her attention focused on the dead snake. I looked at it for a moment, but I was dazzled by its shiny skin in the strong sunshine. As I looked away and up, I couldn't avoid looking at the sun directly, then away to the distant Gweshumba Mountains on the other side of Runde River. For a moment nothing mattered except the possibility of imagination the view always offered me, rolling mountains suggesting things scarier than a harmless baby snake, yet over and over again I would look at them and feel reassured that no matter what, things would work in my favour, that I would study for my exams and pass them, that I would grow up and become whatever I dreamed. Those distant mountains always inspired thoughts of places where dreams were possible, places where I wouldn't have to worry about witches pursuing me.

I blinked and returned my attention to the present moment. And, as if she too had entered a world of her own, Maiguru was still nodding at the lifeless snake. What was she thinking of doing with it — to it? I wasn't going to touch it. She could touch it if she wanted, to be the first one to touch it.

I started to walk away, noiselessly, already planning to finish my reading at Chisiya hill, the quietest of all the places I considered my libraries. Occasionally, I would see snakes in Chisiya, but, other than worrying about my safety, I never thought anything unusual in seeing them. It was I who had invaded their habitat, and as long as I didn't bother them, they would leave me alone. But this one here, coming to me like this, then trying to follow me... that was strange and intolerable. I kicked a pebble to let Maiguru know that I was leaving, so she wouldn't waste her time including me in her plans of what to do with the snake.

At first she didn't seem to have noticed that I was leaving. I started humming a hymn. Soon as I was in the sun, I started sweating, even though there was a slight breeze. I knew I hadn't quite recovered from my recent illness.

I heard Maiguru clear her throat and I turned sharply to see what she was doing. In fact, I shuffled back before she noticed that I had tried to leave. I was interested in seeing what she was going to do next.

"You're lucky you saw it before it entered you," she said calmly. She had sweat beads on her upper lip, a sign that she was really beginning to get worried or angry about something. "Because if you had not seen it in time, we would be talking about a different story right now." She looked at me. "And you wouldn't be standing there pretending all you care about is reading."

"Entering me? What are you talking about now?" I asked her, but she looked away.

I didn't know where this new subject had come from and where it was going, but I wanted to hear more. I didn't recall ever hearing the prophet mentioning the entering part. And her idea, the way she had said it... why was she talking about things entering things? I didn't want my mind to wander to places it shouldn't, but seriously, what was she talking about? I just started laughing, my hand leaning against the wall, as if I was preventing myself from falling with the laughter.

She startled me by saying, "Silly boy. Always full of dirty thoughts."

"Who is thinking about dirty things here?" I wanted to say more, to explain to her how I could easily say that she was the dirty-minded one, but I let her say the next thing. She was the older and mature adult here.

"You forget that that's not the way a junior deacon should behave?" she said and proceeded to shake her head in apprehension.

Oh, that was another thing, my being a junior deacon. It was all new to me, the church, the new position, and now witches sending snakes. Sometimes, thinking too much about my upcoming exams, I forgot about being a deacon. Of course, I was excited about holding such a position in Mototi; I knew others envied me, but school was critical too. Then the prophet, shouldn't he have chosen a better time to tell me about my enemies? I always was one to believe that what you didn't know did not hurt you — something I had read in one of my novels, and it worked. Now I knew too much that could disrupt my studies.

"They are not happy about your intelligence," the prophet had said. He told me that the witches of our village were trying to hurt me before I took my exams; they didn't want me to finish secondary school, didn't want our family to succeed. My elder brother and I were considered foreign in Mototi since we had moved from Mafuva, when I was just a toddler. What was worse, our father, a Shangani man, had migrated from Mozambique, and, although we were born in Zimbabwe, people called us, Mozambicans, and that wasn't a compliment. The prophet said I was beginning to make many people uneasy with my success at school. I was succeeding too fast, as if I had forgotten my station in life.

"But how can they think I have succeeded if I haven't even written the exams," I had asked.

"To them, every step you take when you walk to school is progress," he said. The prophet went on to remind me of the other illnesses I had experienced when I wrote my Grade seven and Junior Certificate exams: there was a pattern. Once he said this, I listened more intently; I was convinced that he had a good spiritual vision; there was no way he could just have known these details; we had not talked about them before the session, he wasn't from Mototi, and I knew no one else had told him that information. I had become a bit scared, yet I was comforted when he delivered instructions on how I could protect myself. Maiguru, who had been kneeling by my side to listen in, had nodded vigorously, her way of reminding me to take the prophet seriously, as if she knew something already about this. I started nodding too, curious to hear more about my future. Something more: I began to feel skin crawling as if I was about to be seized by the same power that gripped the prophet; and I nodded more rapidly and ended up shaking my head side to side until I started feeling dizzy, and the whole time Maiguru was saying "Ameni" with each word the prophet spoke. The prophet told us that the witches were going to be more aggressive this time, since my being a convert in the church was like a challenge to them, a spiritual provocation. They would start with warnings — small snakes — then move on to potent curses.

Maiguru paced about, a worried, or maybe, wise look on her face, her eyes squinting. She hovered near the snake, rotating around it in a ritual I didn't understand. I cared not to understand now; with exams ahead of me, and having barely survived another long illness, all I had time to remember were school-related things. No time to think about snakes entering people.

Maiguru's ritual was beginning to worry me. I moved closer to see what she was doing. When she stopped pacing she said, "I was just trying to tell you that a snake this small can get inside you and live in your stomach, to eat your food. With the way you eat nowadays, I think you already have something in there." She pointed at my stomach with her small finger.

"I eat so much because I didn't eat a lot when I was ill, you know," I said, touching my flat stomach, which started growling. I then remembered that she had food cooking in the kitchen.

"You don't know that," she said, her voice firmer. "Sometimes you have to let yourself know only what those who see what you can't see tell you." She paused to let me react, but I was still waiting to hear where she was going with this. "You must know by now that Madhuveko is considered the best prophet from Nhenga."

"I know," I said.

"You don't," she said, waving at me dismissively. "Because if you did, you wouldn't act the way you are right now."

"It's just that I have to catch up with others at school, and then worry later." Even as I said the words, I saw that they registered their emptiness as frowns on Maiguru's face. She probably thought the illness had done something to my head. She stood there as if she could understand what I was going through better than I, and I hated it. I hated that out of the other students at Gwavachemai Secondary, I was the one who had had to miss school because of illness, and then as if that was not enough, I had to deal with witches and their antics. They had no idea how strong I was: I would not let them scare me out of ambition. I was the best student, and despite all the classes I had missed, I would

120

catch up with and exceed others. They just had no idea. Witches!

"Just worry about catching up when you get to Harare," Maiguru said, her voice hesitant on the word Harare, as if she didn't believe that the transfer would happen. Perhaps she didn't want me to go any more. "For now, you just have to be on the lookout. These signs are real." She turned again and pointed at the one sign lying dead in front of us. "Think about Harare, Babamunini." She then folded her arms across her chest and looked at the cloudless sky. I looked at it too, and we stood like that as if were waiting for Harare to appear like in a dream. But what appeared was an eagle which hovered above for a moment, then floated away. Maiguru quickly looked down at the snake, then away. I opened my book again, tried to read, but instead of seeing Cassius, I saw Harare and I smiled, but the smile turned painful when the thought that the transfer may not happen struck me. I tried but I just couldn't picture myself there yet.

If the transfer to Harare ended up happening, perhaps to a school like Glen View One High — which I had already visited the first time I spent the August holidays in Harare — it might turn out to be a change for the better. Maiguru was correct on my ability to catch up once I arrived in a place where I didn't have to worry about witches. As soon as Mukoma confirmed the date for my move, I was going to be away from Mototi for a long time. It didn't matter that I would leave all my friends here — Tari with his tricks, Dubious with his useful lies, and Mako with his fishing skills — there was some promise of new things in Harare: I was just going to show those city students how brilliant I was and that growing up in the rural areas didn't mean being dumb. I closed the book and started thinking of how I would introduce myself on the first day of class. I would speak in the best English, of course, tell them that I had received top grades — number one — in every class since Form one, and that I planned to maintain those standards. I could just picture the expressions on their faces.

I doubted that I had a snake inside me though, but Maiguru was right about what the prophet from Nhenga — our church's headquarters — had said. He told me that since I had been blessed to recover from my long illness — which had made me miss school for all of February and March — and since I was scheduled to write my exams in June, I had to leave the village for Harare, where Mukoma worked. Either that, or move to Nhenga temporarily, and only return at exam time. The Harare option, which depended on Mukoma finding sense in what the prophet had said, was my best. Nhenga was a beautiful place, full of spiritual promise, but it didn't have the kind of educational inspiration I needed. No disrespect, but of all the youths we had met there, only a few had gone up to Form two in their education. So I would rather go to Harare to compete with those spoiled city students.

The prophet had also explained the cause of the other symptoms of my illness. The headache he said was the work of demons. The stomach ache resulted from eating poisoned food, but the prayers at the church family in Mariwowo had helped heal it, and then there were chest muscles spasms — a witch had inserted snake flesh in my chest while I slept. This, the prophet said, would attract more snakes to follow me, which could pose great danger since there was no telling what harm the snakes would cause and how soon. So, I needed to watch where I walked, where I sat, where I slept, and even where I shat — in case witches stole my waste and use it to put a deadly curse on me. He had not said anything about snakes entering me. Well, maybe he had, but I was still recovering from my illness then and might have dozed and missed some of what he was saying. He might have mentioned it at the height of my head shaking and spiritual saturation. But the details, even for the junior deacon side of me, were dubious. And as a human driven by mere flesh, what was to stop me from doubting, like Thomas, or being a little arrogant like Caesar?

Maiguru jumped and screamed, her kind of scream, a short deep sound like a goat's bleating.

"What happened?" I dashed closer, my hand extended in case I needed to rescue her.

"It shook," she said, covering her mouth with her hand, her eyes opening wider.

"I don't think it moved," I said, drawing even closer, like a man should.

"Burn it!" she said, pointing at it with both hands. "Burn this work of Satan." She started rotating as if the spirit had caught her and she was about to prophesy.

I couldn't tell if she was really afraid, but she was dramatic enough to appear comical. I preferred this side of her than the ever-serious one.

When she stopped jumping she said, "Burn it, Babamunini! Why do you stand there like a donkey?"

"Now you want me to burn it?" I asked. "I thought you wanted to cook it." I started laughing.

"You think you are funny," she said, rolling her eyes. I hated that eye rolling, and she knew I hated it; it always made me think that she thought she was my age and was trying to flirt with me. I often wondered if she could ever be tempted to seduce me. Just a thought I had once had... wondering, as I always did about many things, whether or not what they said about some maigurus was true, those maigurus who were tempted to seduce their babamuninis when their husbands were away for too long. I started scratching my head, and I felt embarrassed by the thought and hoped she hadn't noticed my discomfort. I knew there was no chance of this, her behaving in this way, not even in my dreams. I brushed the dirty thoughts away and pointing at the snake, said, "Seriously, I thought it was your baby."

She opened her mouth and closed it, as if a thought had struck her; then she frowned and looked away. That's when I realised I had gone too far. I bent forward, following her face. "I didn't mean to say that Maiguru," I said, stepping in front of her so she would see the guilt and regret in my eyes.

She raised her face slowly and looked at me with pensive, tired eyes, but didn't say anything. Then she looked away again. A sharp wave of pain shook me and I could feel it spread through my body. My mouth dried and I didn't know what to do. I hadn't meant to say it that way. And she wasn't making it any easier for me. I got in front of her again and looked at her pleadingly. She puckered up her lips, and continued averting her eyes to avoid my stare. She was upset. She wasn't going to forgive me. I wasn't going to feel good about this. I was going to pray about this all day. To cast away the influence of Satan that gave me dirty thoughts. To empty my mouth of all dirty words and fill it with new clean ones. Maiguru walked away from me, stood against the wall where I had been earlier, her eyes downcast.

I shouldn't have made the baby joke; I shouldn't even have mentioned babies. I knew better.

Maiguru's ten-year-marriage to Mukoma had not yielded a baby, which is why she had joined the Zion Christian Church shortly after I did. In fact, I had encouraged her to join; the new church was different from the old one because it practised prophecy and spiritual healing. It believed in miracles. Some people even said it incorporated elements of African spirituality by using some herbs and holy water concoctions to treat physical and spiritual ailments. Most importantly, the church could solve big curses such as infertility. The prophets had told Maiguru that they could solve her problem, and they recommended, commanded even, that she travel to Nhenga, four or five times in a row, each time spending a week or two, in order to become pregnant. They even pointed at women in the congregation who had been in her predicament. The solution anchored on the utilisation of holy forces to ward off evil ones that had padlocked her womb. At first even I had questioned why she had to go to Nhenga, suspecting that the prophets were some kind of infidels, but later I understood that Nhenga operated like the headquarters of healing, and if it had been a hospital, it would have been the main branch, with better facilities. Whole families stayed there for months; those with tough demons, those with mental problems, the blind, the barren — they all converged there. And if Nhenga failed to take care of their problems, they were referred to Mbungo, in the Masvingo Province, where the headquarters of the church was located. In the rarest of occasions, the most difficult problems were referred to Zion City Moria, in South Africa, where the church, headed by the Lekganyane family, originated. South Africa was the ultimate Mecca for members of our church, and the place all stubborn ailments were treated. So there was going to be a solution for Maiguru's problem of many years, but like me, she had to check with Mukoma first before she considered travelling to Nhenga.

Maybe Mukoma would ask me to accompany her to Nhenga, which would dash my dreams of transferring to Harare. The worst that could happen was that he would beat both of us for following the orders of strangers — he always argued with Apostolic Faith members whenever they tried to preach to him, and often, he ended up being the one explaining religion to them, warning them of its cousins: oppression, poverty, and injustice. As far as I knew, he had not disapproved of my following of ZCC, but I was afraid he might not allow me to go either to Harare or Nhenga, and probably would tell me to leave the church altogether. Maiguru's worst fear was always that he would be infuriated and take a second wife. Or a third one since she suspected he already had another in the city where he spent more time than he did in the village. I knew he sometimes lived with a woman I had met when I had gone to Harare in August last year, but he had instructed me not to mention her to Maiguru or to anyone. He might even have told me that he thought the woman was pregnant, but I hadn't paid attention to that detail—I was infuriated that the woman had the audacity to take the place of my Maiguru. Of course, I had not told Maiguru, and now I could not tell her something I wasn't sure of anymore. What was important was that Maiguru do what she needed to do in order to be fertile. She had told me that she would go to Nhenga no matter what, even if that meant secretly, and I couldn't blame her.

Suddenly, Maiguru's eyes shone with life again, as if she had been struck by a new realisation. She looked at me and smiled. I felt new warmth occupy my body, and I wanted to hug her right there. Instead, I cleared my throat and said, "I'm sorry."

"Sorry for what?" she asked, and started walking away.

"I didn't mean what I said." I followed her, not caring about the snake anymore.

She stopped, turned and said, "You didn't say anything." She widened her smile.

I smiled too. I had decided to listen to everything she was going to say, letting her take as much time as she wanted. Reading could wait.

"Burn the snake, Babamunini," she said. "Show them they don't have power over you."

"I'll do so right away, to shame them," I said, offering her my book, which she waved away. I wanted to remind her that she had wanted to be the first one to touch it, but I said, "I'm going to light up a fire right away."

"No, just pour paraffin and light a match. Delaying will cause its mother to smell its death and come after you. And you don't want that to happen now, do you?"

"That makes great sense, Maiguru," I said. "I like your idea of dousing it in paraffin."

She resumed walking and left me standing there as she rushed back into the kitchen. Just before entering the hut she, without stopping or turning, said, "Hurry up too, or I will finish all the food."

126

"Food!" I shouted, and scurried towards the firewood pile. Just then I realised how hungry I was.

The thing didn't take time to burn. I buried the ashes in the sweet potato plot; then I took my book and entered the kitchen hut where a plate of sadza and catfish waited for me. Maiguru laughed at me when I closed the door tightly, but before she followed up her laughter with a remark, I said, "I'm ready for the next one."

Even though she didn't say anything immediately, I knew somewhere in the middle of the meal, she would raise the issue of my remark. The talk to follow might take longer than I could afford, but I didn't have to read all night. I would get the opportunity to apologise properly. In the meantime, I would eat and keep my mind away from snakes and the fact that this was possibly the first of many visits to come.

Emmanuel Sigauke is a Zimbabwean writer based in Sacramento, California, where he teaches English and Creative Writing at Cosumnes River College. He has published poetry and prose in numerous magazines, and co-edits *Cosumnes River Journal, Munyori Literary Journal*, and *African Roar*. He is the author of *Forever Let Me Go* a poetry collection, and writes online at *Wealth of Ideas*.

Out of Memory

Emmanuel Iduma

He thinks, while he is leaving, that Ella defies the law of gravity. She goes up with ease and does not return; she goes up and does not know the way down, her body is unaccustomed to return. She is looking at the curtain, window, or wind; for he can tell that she has undertaken a journey, and she might not return. But why does he think of all this? He is with her, in a room he once entered when it was her sister he knew. The room in its present state does not exist in his memory. In her sister's days it had brightly coloured curtains, the wall was adorned with wallpapers, and there was a Butterfly sewing machine. All that is gone. The room bears a new occupant, the curtains are white, and there are no wallpapers. It has been repainted; and only has a bed, stool, and white curtains. He is sitting on the stool. She is sitting on the bed. She is looking at the curtain, window, or wind.

Ella's mother comes to him. It is the day before.

"She called your name. Frank. Frank Duru."

She says it like Ella must've said it. There is confidence in her voice, but he knows it's a superficial confidence. She proves this; tears run down her cheeks after she calls his name.

"Don't worry Ma," he responds, touching her shoulder lightly; in his memory she's a woman with an overflowing contagious hate.

"Don't tell me don't worry. When you see her you'll know I should worry." Then she adds, "Would you come?"

He wants to think about Ella calling his name, in place of thinking about going to Ella. It's a useless thought, he surmises, so he says, "Yes." And she holds him firmly, both her hands on his arms.

"God bless you, Frank."

Frank could have asked her what's important about his presence, as was usual with him. He loses the guts to do so, and instead looks at her and says, "Yes," again. The CD player is playing a Michael Buble song, which he thinks is inappropriate for the moment. But he thinks of this only after Ella's mother has closed his door, walking away in the rain, as she came. Then he sits down, forgetting what he had wanted to remember, and begins to think the rain is a healing balm, for all of them.

Ella's elder sister, Beatrice, comes to Frank before she leaves for Abuja, the day before her mother visits him. His stint with Beatrice, as they say, is a long story. As a good story, it has its relevant contours, a beginning and a climax, but as a bad story it has no denouement. He goes to the door when he hears a knock and finds that it is Beatrice who had knocked; not a knock but a pat, a rap like a mouse seeking escape from an enemy. For when he sees her again — three years after she had gone away, without as much as a goodbye hug, kiss, or touch — he keeps his gaze away from her eyes, fixes it on the floor. He hears the trees rustle, almost musically. It's a music he thinks she cannot hear.

"Won't you let me in?" she says sharply, though with a smile.

"Beatrice. It's you."

He walks briskly and sits down while she enters, as though being chased by their past. There are only two long couches in his parlour, a CD player but no television or video, a shelf where he keeps the books he bought and has not read — his anti-library. His study is in another room. Beatrice goes to the shelf. She touches the books. Although this occurs in silence — since Beatrice and Frank have no ready words to start a conversation — there is goodly noise to the silence, and the appropriateness of no one saying anything.

"I missed you," she says, still looking at the books, like a character that has been trapped in a story seeking return.

"Oh," he says.

"What?" Beatrice asks, taking her eyes from the books, looking at him.

"I said oh."

"You still say oh? You've not changed."

"Not much."

She leaves the books, the trapped character, walks to the opposite couch and sits.

"I missed you," she says.

This time he says, "Of course," meaning he has missed her too. "How's your husband?"

"Fine."

The last time he saw her husband, Ella was with him in his car.

"How's Ella?"

Beatrice looks into his eyes, and then looks away. "She has a lot of regard for you."

"I know" He nods, and then smiles.

Beatrice smiles too.

"She has a problem."

"What?"

"She speaks to no one. She eats very little. But she keeps writing in her diary. And she allows no one to read it."

"What happened to her?"

"I can't say. I don't know."

Beatrice's eyes betray her; it's obvious she knows the happenstances, every single chain of events leading to her sister's absurdity, but for a reason he cannot pinpoint she doesn't seem to want to say.

"What do you want me to do?"

"Go to her. See if she'd talk to you."

"Oh," he says, and she stands. Her standing seems to him like an act of anger, but he concludes it is an act of guilt. His presence appears to incriminate her, to feed her guilt, and to fan it to flame.

"Please talk to her for me. She might listen to you."

He stands and faces her, saying, "I missed you." But he is not keen about pushing his emotion further, so he suppresses the memories. There was a family meeting that had sealed their fates — sealed them off — so that they stand before each other now as different people, disjointed, not man and wife as he had wished.

As she makes her way to the door, he feels compelled to sit. She does not turn to him, nor for once look back. When he looks at the door and sees her backside, he thinks she is moving as though in a trance.

He says to Ella, "I am here." This is the second time he has come to her. She said nothing to him the first time, only looking at the window or the wind. It seemed, then, that she had a penchant for nothingness, for void. But today there is a display of colour on her face. She turns to him. The diary is beside her pillow, within reach of her hands. He smiles when their eyes meet, but her eyes are not the eyes they used to be. Her eyes always seemed to question without asking questions. But unlike the days he taught her, she has no enquiry in her eyes. Instead, there is listlessness, brownish listlessness.

He says again, "I am here."

She keeps looking at him with that brownish listlessness. Then it calcifies to brownish temperance, and then brownish mercy. This is when he feels she would talk to him.

She says, "I can only talk about the man. Nothing else."

He makes a mistake before he realises he is making it. He asks, like a refrain to her words, "Which man?" She takes her brownish mercy from him. The swiftness with which she turns her eyes from him, is to him like being tied to a stake, being punished for heresy. He feels blasphemous; he feels he is a grand blasphemer.

Now she holds her diary, swiftly turning the pages, deftly even. She starts to write furiously when she gets to a blank page. He stands to leave, still feeling blasphemous, but she does not notice. Frank knows what he will think about. The man.

Beatrice calls him that evening. He is surprised she still has his phone number, or could call him. This is the first time she has called in three years. Frank has always imagined her voice at the other end of the line, re-enacted it. But now, saying 'hello' and hearing her voice, he can't remember what he had expected her voice to sound like, or the response he'd planned to give.

"Beatrice?"

"Yes."

"How are you?"

"Good. Good."

"Oh. That's good." He resists the temptation to say 'good' a second time.

"I'm back in Abuja. I thought I should call, you know. Find out how things are going with you."

"Oh. Very good."

Then, words cease. He feels he can hear the breath from her mouth – the way it sounds makes him think it's not from her nostrils.

"It's good you called."

"Yes. How's Ella?"

He does not want to tell her. He feels, somewhat, that he is a therapist, or a psychotherapist who values confidentiality.

"Frank?"

"Oh. She's fine."

"She has talked to you?"

It is, now, a matter of yes or no. "No," he says. His thinking is that there are lies better suited to reality than truths.

"I have something to tell you. I have not been honest with you."

133

Those are the same words she said three years ago; before she told him there was someone else, another man, a soldier who'd recently divorced. They have been there before — that place with undiluted déjà vu.

"What?"

"It's about Ella. I think I know what caused this."

"Okay."

He hears her breathe from her mouth again. It sounds laboured, intense, as though she has just taken a dose of Verapamil.

"I'll talk to you later. Tomorrow."

He nods, and although he knows she cannot see him nodding he is convinced that she is nodding, too.

Ella's mother meets him at the door. She has a towel around her neck, and is holding a jar without water. She smiles — she looks obese, as though her smile is an inflating machine; it has much significance for Frank. He recognises her moods by her size. In anger, she is gangly. In appeal and want she is medium-sized, in-between. But in joy she is obese, as she is today.

He smiles in return.

She says, "Ah. Frank. She ate well last night, and this morning."

Now in the parlour he loses touch with what she is saying, and thinks backward. In the parlour he is now standing he once sat three and a half years ago with his mother and brother. Ella's mother had said, "I can't let her marry you. There is someone better for her." Then she left them without another word — and he looked at his mother and brother to measure their disappointment, and anger. But he is here; he is back to the place he was banished from, at the service of the woman who'd banished him.

"Frank?"

"Oh yes," he replies, looking startled.

"You are doing so much for me."

"Oh."

"Yes."

"It's not a problem. She's still my student."

"Don't mock me. You forget how long ago she left your school?"

"She's my student."

"Oh. Sit down."

He sits, and she sits beside him. He thinks he can perceive the faint smell of fresh baking.

"How is it going these days? I hear the standards are falling."

He sees that she is nervous. "Sure. The standards have fallen. But we do what we have to do."

"Yes? What is it you teach again?"

"Philosophy."

"Ella was a philosophy student?"

"Yes."

"For three years?"

"Yes. I taught her in her second and third year."

"Oh. I remember. Those were difficult times."

"Yes."

There is silence. For each of them the memory comes rushing in like a torrent. Each time they try to forget, to think instead of the present.

"Do you want anything? Before you go to her?"

"No. I'm fine."

"Not food? Not water? I made pancakes, you know."

"I'm fine, Ma. Thank you."

Then he goes in. He walks into Ella's room again, into the white walls and white curtains, and perhaps, into the wind.

Ella says, the moment his gaze meets hers, "He was so kind. We talked before we undressed. We talked."

He sits beside her on the bed. He perceives the fresh scent of bathing soap. And he listens. But she speaks no further; she is only smiling. He had not previously noticed her gaptooth, or what seemed like a multitude of teeth in her mouth, and the smallness of her teeth.

"We undressed. But we talked. I undressed him. He undressed me. But we talked."

Frank does not know why, but he says, "Okay. That's good."

"Yes good. Yes good. You know him?"

"Him?"

"Yes. Him."

Good Lord, Frank Duru thinks. "No."

"They talk about him everyday in the news." She points to a radio, which he has just seen for the first time in the room. He cannot tell why he'd not seen it earlier, although it is on the table. "But you say you don't know him?"

"Yes."

"He undressed me and you say you don't know him?"

"Yes."

"Yes yes yes. You keep saying yes. Please say no. Say no. Say no. Please say no." And she starts to cry. He moves close to her and holds her.

The door opens, her mother is there.

Ella says, "He didn't say no to me. He said yes. Yes. Yes…"

Her mother just stands there, looking flummoxed. Frank lulls her, until she stops crying, until she places her head on his shoulder, and says, "I think of him when I see you. You hold me like he did. Don't leave me."

"Oh. Okay."

He returns to his house in the dark, while the noise of a radio lingers in his head. He has no radio in his house, but he knows the news. He hears it everywhere. Or, at least, he knows the news that matters. Yet, he cannot figure the man who Ella said was talked about in the news every day. The man has entered his thoughts, resident like a leech, and he does not know how to dislodge it. So when Beatrice calls, although it is almost midnight, he says, "Ella keeps talking about a man."

"I have called a thousand times. Where have you been?"

"With Ella. She said she thinks of him when she sees me. Who is he? I know you know."

There is silence like a monster, feeding on his heart, and maybe on Beatrice's, for Frank thinks he can hear her body quivering.

"Beatrice?"

"Yes."

"Talk to me. You can talk to me."

"Yes. I know. I need to talk."

"Talk then."

"My husband's friend was an aide of the head of state."

"What head of state?"

"The same head of state."

"The dead one?"

"Yes."

"Oh. Oh God."

"You must know that I didn't ask Ella to leave school. She left on her own. She said she was bored of school. I think she made up her mind one holiday she visited Abuja. When she met Ade. Ade changed everything. Ella called my husband and told him to come and get her. I don't know what Ade told her, what he said to convince her. But I think my husband knew. He was in it from the start. That was why she called him. He told me, one night, that he was travelling the next day to get Ella. I asked him why. He said it was none of my business. I said nothing because it seemed he was in a bad mood. I know what he can do in a bad mood. Ella shows up in my house, and greets me like a stranger. The next morning she is out. That is the last time I saw her before she is brought back, in her present state."

"Oh."

"What is this oh? I tell you all these things and the best you can say is oh? Oh?"

"Well, what do you want me to say?" He is angry; he does not know why.

"Say nothing."

"I'm sorry," he says, but cannot tell why he is sorry for what he said in anger, or if he should be the one saying sorry.

"I overheard Ade saying to my husband that he took her to the head of state. The man wanted girls. He said she'd spend two nights with him. And they laughed about it. Frank, they laughed about it."

"Was she with him that night?" He asked, but she ended the conversation and the line went dead. Yet he held the receiver to his ear still, waiting for her to speak.

Frank does not go to university the next morning. Aside from the possibility of a lecture-free day, given the protesting students — who are claiming the death of the head of state should end military rule — he needs to talk to Ella again. He does not want to believe, or conceive, that Ella had been with the head of state the night he died. When he gets to the door of Ella's mother's house, his memory regurgitates her name twice, Mrs. Anjola, Mrs. Anjola. He had dispensed with it, discarded the name when he knew he wasn't getting married to Beatrice. But now it comes out of his memory, as if forgetting it in the first place was fruitless.

Mrs. Anjola meets him at the door. She is smiling. She is her inflated self, again. "Come in," she says, holding the door. He has barely entered when she says, from behind him, "Sit down."

He thanks her and sits. He is nervous with impatience. He does not need a discussion with Mrs. Anjola. He needs to talk to Ella.

She sits, beside him. "Did you ever meet my husband?"

"No."

"But you heard about what he did to us?"

"Yes. Beatrice told me."

"That's right. So you heard how he left us for that woman, that Major's wife?"

"Yes."

"And how they had a quarrel and he tried to come back to me but I refused, I shut the door on him?"

"No. I didn't hear that part."

"That's the best part. I don't give second chances. No man messes with me. You know that?"

"Yes. I know that."

She smiles. Frank smiles too. His impatience, though, increases. He does not see the point of her recollection.

"Do you know how he died?"

"No."

"Ah. The devil gives with one hand and takes with the other. He went back to her when I refused him. And her husband caught them in the act. The Major was furious. He shot my husband dead right there on the bed. You don't joke with an army man. We heard he did not wait for an explanation. He did not wait for my husband to beg. He pulled his gun and shot."

"Oh."

She shakes her head in mock pity. "It changed my life. I lost focus." She turned to him, looking at him in the eye. "But I needed to take care of my girls. I needed money. I refused you because I didn't think you had money." She pauses, as though waiting to see the effect of her revelation. "The Army man came. I said yes." She pauses again, so that to Frank her words seems like a measuring tape, her pauses are the numbers marked on it. "I made a mistake. I'm sorry. Do you hear me?"

"Yes."

"I'm sorry. It should have been you. I should have said yes to you."

He does not know what to think, or say. He is not prepared for this. In his memory, that dreamed part of it, there is no apology from Mrs. Anjola. As such, he is thrust onstage without rehearsal. "Let me go to Ella. I need to talk to her." He stands. She stands with him.

"Okay," she says. "You heard what I said?"

"Yes. Yes."

She nods, and seems inflated again. "She spoke to me yesterday. After you left."

"What did she say?"

"She said I shouldn't worry about her."

"Oh. That's good. Good. Good."

"Yes. Good."

Ella is standing when he enters. Her diary is in her hand. The radio is on, but its volume is low. She has her back to the door. She is staring at the white curtains, window, or both, or the wind. Frank goes to her and touches her lightly on the shoulder. She turns. "They're going to have elections," she says, looking at him.

"Who are they?"

"They."

"The head of state?"

"He's one of them. He's not the man."

"Is he new?"

"New?"

"Yes. New."

"Yes. No. New? Yes."

"Sit down."

She sits. She has not taken her eyes from him. "You want to undress me?"

"What did he do to you?"

"He undressed me. I can show you how."

"No," he says, with spite. He calms down. He cannot afford to lose his cool. "What happened after he undressed you?"

"What happened?"

"Yes."

"Nothing happened."

"What happened to him?"

She takes her eyes off him, looking around the room as though in search of something.

"What happened to him," Frank asks again; this time he is more firm. He's thinking that this moment will be significant, when considered in retrospect.

"What happened to him?"

"Yes."

"What about me? Something happened to me."

"I want to know what happened to him."

She starts to cry. Frank does not pull her to him, or calm her. Instead he screams out, "What happened to him?"

The noise of her crying and Frank's shout brings her mother; she stands at the door, as though in supplication. Frank holds both of her shoulders and shakes her, violently, as though he wants to force it out of her memory. "Tell me what happened to him!"

"I don't know. He was mad. He danced around the room, naked, he was shouting. It seemed like there was fire on him." When Frank says nothing, she says, "What did I do? Why did he die after undressing me? After touching my breasts? I swear, I swear, he did not sleep with me. He wanted to. But that was when he started dancing and shouting. He touched his head and his buttocks, then his stomach and chest. There were tears in his eyes and spittle in his mouth. And he fell on the floor. He fell on the floor and did not stand again. Do you know why he fell and died?"

Frank remembers the popular saying that it was an act of God – God had dispensed the dictator, thrust him away like waste. But he cannot say it; it sounds farfetched, mystic, surreal, and unnecessary. "I don't know."

"You don't know? You don't know? You keep asking to know what happened to him. I tell you and you say you don't know why? You don't know why?" She starts to cry again. This time Mrs. Anjola comes to the bedside. She stands beside Ella, doing nothing. Frank stands; he is feeling useless and dumb. And he is thinking that he'll always be worthless – she has told him the truth and he does nothing about it.

His phone rings as he enters his house. The journey has been longer, perhaps because he is feeling ashamed.

"Frank?" asks Beatrice. "What happened? You're sounding sick."

"She told me. I could not tell her why he died."

"The Head of State?

"Yes."

There is a pause. Then she asks, slowly, her words like drops of drizzling rain, "Is that a problem? How many things can you explain?"

"Do not philosophise me."

She laughs. "You teach philosophy. How can I try to philosophise you?"

"I really don't want to talk."

"You need to talk. You must talk."

"To you?"

"Yes. To anybody. To me."

"Okay."

She laughs again. "I'm coming back."

"When?"

"Friday."

"It's two days away. You're in a hurry?"

"I'm leaving him."

"You are leaving him?"

"Yes. He has promised to leave the Army. You know, retire. Go into politics, now that the acting head of state has promised to hand over to a civilian government. I told him I don't care. He tried to threaten me. I said he can go to hell."

"Oh. That should count for something."

"You say oh again. Oh. Oh. Oh."

"Oh. That's funny."

She laughs, on and on, as though she has been smoking a spliff.

"You're happy."

"Yes. I'm coming back. I'm free."

"From what? Free from what?"

"Nothing. But I'm free. I feel free."

He laughs, like her, on and on.

"You're happy too."

"Oh. Yes. And I don't know why."

So they laugh together, on and on. He can't tell who replaces the receiver first.

He runs all the way to Mrs. Anjola's house. She spoke to him on the phone; there was urgency in her voice. But when he gets to the door, which is slightly open, he can hear the radio, loud and clear, as though the demodulator is fixed in the room. He walks into Ella's room. Mrs. Anjola is there, on the bed. Ella is writing in her diary.

"Frank. You're here," Mrs. Anjola says. "She says she wants you to see her notes. Her diary. She wants you to confirm if she has the right notes." She is sobbing while speaking; her tears are flowing freely, as though if she cries longer her tears will form a lagoon.

Frank sits beside Ella. She does not raise her head. She is writing furiously, quickly — it appears to Frank that she is on the verge of death and writing an imperceptible message.

"Ella," says Frank.

She adds a full stop and gives him the diary. Her handwriting is nearly illegible, but distinct — no one else would be able to write like her. She is smiling. There is a full page of fresh writing. The first lines are, "Whereof we cannot speak, thereof we must be silent. Philosophy, therefore, is dead."

He knows it has come out of her memory; the part of her memory when he taught her, the first class, when he announced those words as a precursor to the study of philosophy, the essence of philosophy. He reads no further.

"You want to return?" Frank asks.

"Return?"

"To the university?"

"No."

"No?"

"Yes."

"Yes?"

"Yes."

"Oh. Okay."

Mrs. Anjola is still sobbing, she is not looking at any of them; she seems to be sobbing about something in her memory. But Ella is smiling; she is looking at the white curtains or the wind, or both. And Frank, recalling his last conversation with Beatrice, wants to laugh again. He can hear the radio. It's loud and clear.

Emmanuel Iduma, born in Nigeria, holds a degree in Law and will be called to the Nigerian Bar in January 2012. Aside from *Saraba* which he co-publishes, his writing has appeared elsewhere online and in print. He is participating in the Invisible Borders Trans-African Photography Project 2011, and will realise other self-sponsored residencies and projects across Africa in 2012. At present, he is working on a novel and keeping a beard.

Diner Ten

Ivor Hartmann

"It is we who rule this earth, don't let anyone tell you otherwise. We have existed, simply, in our present modern form for over 150 million years, and only it took us 3.8 billion years to get there from virtually single-celled organisms. Every other multi-celled organism on our planet, including humans, is as far as we are concerned, just passing through..." — Master-Teacher Tagam.

Radic squeezed through a gap in an air-vent. His passage and that of the millions before him had burnished it smooth and bright around its edges. Inside the lobby it was dark and greasy from the cooking that took place below. Radic quietly took his place in the line of diners. From this point on there would be silence; battle-rules applied until one exited again, hopefully alive and well-fed. This diner, Diner Ten, was well known for both its safety and good food. It had been home to some catastrophes, but they were few and far between, and its local council safety rating was on average very good, a four-point-five out of five at present if he wasn't mistaken.

As he usually did when waiting for something to happen, Radic drifted into daydreams. A habit from youth he knew bordered on the ridiculous, especially now that he was middle-aged and pretty much knew how the rest of his life would turn out. His society had strict rules and laws; everyone had something to do, a purpose, which kept it going.

A tap on the leg brought him out of the depths. Turning around he saw Gradulk, a long-time friend; they were born in adjoining nursery cells. Gradulk waved his limp antennae in a silent hello, and then mimed let's get a drink after dinner. Radic agreed with a crisp salute, and they both smiled.

146

A brisk shake of his shoulder, and Radic was being forcefully guided to the entrance. A soldier surged him forward, pulled him to an abrupt stop at the threshold, and for some reason gave him a bitter glare. The soldier held one tibia in front of Radic and signalled his buddies for a go response with his antennae. Radic wondered about the soldier's rudeness, but the smell of the feasts wafting through the entrance grabbed his attention and his belly growled. The soldier gave him another bitter glance, but before Radic could respond, the soldier's tibia was at his back, and he was nearly flung through the entrance.

Radic screeched to a halt and took stock of his surroundings. He was cautious by nature, and it had saved his life many times. All was quiet, only the steady hum of a refrigerator filled the diner. All was dark; well, for humans anyway, which generally meant they weren't in the diner. He stood still for a bit longer, breathing deep the rich scents. On the far range of his hearing, he could make out the ever-so-quiet movements of his fellow diners.

Still cagey, he high-tailed it to his favourite starting point; the pots left over from the most recent meal. They were sitting in the sink, and as usual, filled with water to the brim. This was Radic's hors d'oeuvre, and he crept happily into the damp sink and up the dented pot to the edge of the brimming water.

Always one to savour the moment, he took the barest sip and let it swish around his mouth. For a moment his saliva spurted painfully, as the bold flavour of a mutton curry swirled in a glorious symphony bombarding his senses. Closing his eyes in rapture he let it all drip slowly down his throat and explode warmly in his stomach. Even from within Radic's blind rapture he heard Gradulk scurry past; his distinct one leg slightly scraping on each off-step from an old war wound. Gradulk would be headed to the bread bin first; he always liked to start with fresh bread if it was available. Suddenly, that he knew his friend's intimate habits so well brought a sour note into his savouring. It smacked of too many years gone by with no change, no change, just a slow inexorable passage along a path too wide and straight, to the grave.

Radic took another sip and started to repeat the process. But the bold pleasure was gone, along with his semi-good mood and he just swallowed it all in a gulp. Relishing the storm of curry fire in his stomach, almost as a deserved punishment, he leapt from the pot onto the main kitchen counter.

It wasn't the smartest thing to be doing; he should have gone the long way around in the darkest safety; the normal route behind the tall stacks of rarely-moved containers that lined the back of the counter. There was a momentary surprised scrabbling from the other diners at his disregard for well-known survival rules. Radic didn't care; all he wanted was a bit of that old brown sugar, one slightly crystallised step away from lapsing back into treacle. That would cheer him right up, he hoped.

The vast and powerful overhead light came on. A blinding flash so strong he thought he could see through his exoskeleton for a moment. It felt like a god had pulled the real sun into the room to hang above him; and great though his fear and light-loathing were, he froze. This, instinct said, would provide him an initial invisibility.

Radic waited for the blindness to fade until he could make out the new human of this dwelling. It was the one who arrived two years ago to join the one who had lived alone up until then. He released a slow, soundless sigh of relief but remained motionless. This human rarely attacked on sight; the chances were one in three thousand, according to the recent stats in the *Windsor Daily*.

The human lurched to the sink and began to wash a mug. Radic zoomed as fast as his limbs could carry him across the counter to the stacked containers. First, he dove for the narrow shadow presented by a container's curved base. Then he crawled to a gap between one container and another. With one last look over his shoulder, he saw the human turn and come towards him. Radic whipped himself into the dark gap and ran halfway to the back, before the human's shadow swept past.

Fool, you old bloody fool, Radic thought as he wheezed from his exertions and came to a stop. He leant on the wall to catch his breath, and saw from the corner of his eye three diners scuttling past. Their rigid antennas shook solemnly at his actions, but they wouldn't join his foolishness by commenting. Radic felt almost mortified enough to start ecdysis right then and there. Leave behind his exuvium and as an anonymous soft and gooey teneral, escape. He could already imagine the whispers: There goes Radic. Do you know what he did at Diner Ten? Right in front of the whole dining crowd? No! Yes!

What a fool, he added to himself once again, but why? What made him so reckless besides the obvious boredom, nostalgia, and thoughts of his own mortality? The humans' kettle wailed and he focused on that; better than facing these questions that stung his mind.

Footfalls, a brief shadow across the strip of light reflected on the wall aside him.

A tinkle, scrape, waterfall of boiling water, rapid tinkling as the human stirred his mug of tea, a final clink on the edge of his mug, and the human would get the milk from the fridge. Radic predicted through pure rote, and sure enough there came the first tinkle.

If humans were so predictable, he pondered, were we just as so to them? Sure they had, and still did, study his kind in detail. Living so close together it was inevitable, but what did our actions tell them about us really? Did they know all beings lived, loved, and died, just as they did, with the full awareness as conscious beings within the scope of their present form? Of course, humans were chasms apart from his kind in their perception of reality. But we all shared the same basic drives as did all life forms. In many ways modern humans had been a boon for his kind. Especially in cities stuffed full by wanton excess thrown away seemingly on whim. They even gathered it into huge mountains of ripe for the picking. Sure there was the occasional price to pay, hence the diner ratings, but on the whole, his urban kind had never lived better.

Radic realised he was in a nice thick darkness again, the human must have turned off the light and left. He hadn't even noticed the change, and that worried him some; the diner was not a place to be woolgathering in. Wearily, he stood straight, brushed his antennae and set out along the safe path towards the top shelf of Cupboard Four. He was going to get some solid good food, he had decided, none of that brown sugar blow-your-mind-crap tonight.

The couscous was delicious. Radic ate from the thick dust filtered down over time, caused by the weevils eating away above. There were a few others with his appetite for the same dust, and they nodded hello as they crawled their way along the pathways at the bottom of the box. The couscous had been here for just over a year and a half, used once and then forgotten at the very back of Cupboard Four. He ate his full and some more; to stock up and weather the upcoming drinking session with Gradulk a bit better.

Radic furtively scampered back to the entrance of Diner Ten. He nipped through the entrance into the darkness, barely missing a waiting guest held in place by the same soldier, who looked up and gave him the same look as before. Radic almost responded, but saw Gradulk impatiently waiting at the air-vent exit and hurried to meet him.

They walked in silence as old friends do comfortably, under the rooftop beams in the attic making their way towards the bar. Radic was still irked by that soldier; if he saw him again he would give him a piece of his mind, not for nothing had he too served. He had killed for his kin's wellbeing, survived horrors that wiped out his fellow infantrymen by the tens of thousands, and well, he deserved a bit more respect. Sure, he had been a fool for a moment in Diner Ten but hadn't they all at some point. He had survived, alive and intact, and that's what mattered ultimately. If Gradulk had seen or heard the debacle he gave no sign of it, but that was Gradulk's nature.

The bar Heat was built under a huge old water heater and so named for the pleasant heat it generated year round. The heater loomed above them and gave a low groan of cold water coming in, as if to welcome them. Radic felt the heat rise long before he could see the actual bar and by the time they were underneath, it was positively tropical. Heat was run by the brothers Dankle and Thurd. Their micro breweries were strung high above their establishment, along the heater's sweltering sides. If he looked up carefully, Radic could just see them in the distant gloom; a spider-web of ladders, leathery brewery kettles, and the small moving dots of the constantly attending brewers. There were many pipes that ran down like spaghetti, along the side, plunging into the flat roof of Heat.

Inside, they were instantly smothered by the wonderful gloomy and steamy atmosphere of Heat. There was the mass hum of fellow drinkers, the pungent scent of impending sex, and copious amounts of spilled and sweated beer. Radic had met his first wife here he remembered — with a twinge of nostalgic panic — as they pushed their way to the bar counter. The combined sweat and breath of the three hundred or so gathered inside, condensed and streamed down the walls to be caught by gutters along the floor edges. Sent then who knows where, probably right up and into new beer kettles, Radic suspected. His kin were not ones to let any renewable resource go to waste.

Gradulk took the lead and used his bigger bulk to force a slow but determined passage, and had already ordered before Radic managed to get through. They looked at each other in silence waiting for the beers. Presently their drinks were slung down the smooth bar in their plastic bubbles and came sliding to a stop at Gradulk's tibia resting on the bar top. They pushed their way out and into a less packed area in the bar extremes. There was a small open table near the far wall, they settled down and Gradulk handed Radic a beer.

"Cheers," Gradulk said, and proceeded to nip the plastic bubble and suck down half the contents with a big squeeze.

Radic followed suit and relished the warm tart flavour. No-one knew exactly what went into the brothers' beer — and most knew better than to ask. Like the mutton curry before it, the beer exploded into a warm glow, but this time shortly after it hit his brain too. The golden glow of the alcohol and whatever, soon tinged his perception with a soft light and calm he had not felt since he had woken up that day.

"So what's bothering you, compadre?" asked Gradulk gently, before he took another squeeze of beer.

"That my old friend... is the right and good question," Radic grunted.

"Meaning you are asking yourself that question already and haven't come up with any satisfactory answers, or justifications that stick," retorted Gradulk. "So what's new Radic, we know no more about ourselves than we did when we were born. Doomed to live and die as what we have become with our consent. I have to believe that we have, and do, fulfil some small part towards the continued existence of our civilisation, every... every... every..."

"Day," finished Radic impatiently as he saw Gradulk was struggling to find the word. "Schoolyard rhetoric Gradulk, that's what you're giving me?" He protested, and his eyes seemed to smoulder, the calm of the beer forgotten. "As useless as all those dreams of glory we were filled with. The great battles we would fight come our time. And what did we get? Nothing but pain, anguish, and raw mental scars that never heal. And, oh yes, a medal. And the rest of our lives waiting in lines. Waiting for our food, water, wives, children, work, and even our own births and deaths are spent in queues waiting for hospital wardrooms and surgeries."

Radic slammed four claws on the table top and drew a few eyes towards him. Gradulk quickly reached out and held Radic's limbs on the table. He looked deep into Radic's eyes to quieten the demons raging inside his friend. It worked like it always did. Radic quickly returned to himself again and smiled weakly at Gradulk, who let go, lent back, and squeezed the last drops from his beer bubble.

"Hang quiet for a moment, I'll fetch us another... another... another... round," Gradulk said, and threw his parched bubble to the floor. He stood and patted Radic's shoulder before heading back into the crowd.

Radic watched him disappear. What had he done to deserve this other man's respect and forbearance, he ruminated. Besides saving Gradulk's life a few times on the battlefield, as had Gradulk in turn saved Radic's many times more, there was nothing else Radic could think of that made him worthy. Gradulk spent his work time helping as an orderly in a hospital, all Radic did was write bad puff pieces for the local rag. Even as a child, Gradulk had been big for his age and he had taken on a role as protector of the weak.

During the wars he had been a supernaturally good medic. That was until the Grand Breaks Offensive, where Gradulk had been captured and nearly eaten alive by an Ampulicidae Wasp. By the slimmest of chances, the wasp sting that first downed him missed his bundle of thorax nerve ganglions by a single antennae width. Gradulk had feigned paralysis and by some miracle the wasp did not sting him again. It was usual for them to sting a second time, right into the brain, and thereby eliminating the impulse to flee. He was dragged by the wasp to its nearby burrow and stacked next to other victims of the long battle, and the wasp left to rejoin the fight. The others were mostly dead, some still dying, but he managed to haul out two of the most likely survivors anyway. Hauled them he did, right through the battlefield into friendly territory, and finally to an emergency medical tent. Before he succumbed to the poison coursing through his body and collapsed comatose for the next three weeks.

That was Gradulk, a natural born hero; one of those guys who ran towards a catastrophe. But when he did finally awake, not all of him came back. His hands shook when he needed them to be still, he couldn't recall the right words of the most ordinary things; like day, beer, or blue. Gone was the hope of earning a medical doctorate through his field service, and a bright and promising career. Though like the hero he was, he took it well and instead became a hospital orderly.

The next beer slapped Radic flat in the face, and like a flap of warm flesh, peeled off and fell to the table. He looked up to see Gradulk grinning madly at him, still working his way back through the crowd. His one arm was crooked and cradled a pile of new beer bubbles; his free claw squeezed the life out of another. Radic had to admit these beer bubbles were pure genius on the part of the brothers; the humans used them for wrapping breakables in transport.

Radic picked up the bubble and toasted Gradulk as he sat down. He nipped and squeezed hard and gulped down three large mouthfuls. Gradulk piled what must have been at least another twelve beer bubbles in the middle of the table. It was becoming apparent to Radic they had quite an evening ahead of them, and he did not mind this at all.

The roar of the attic water heaters wrenched him from a deep slumber. It must be near nightbreak, the beginning of his day, when humans came home from their schools and workplaces. He felt the stillness of those arrayed around him in a dedicated sleep area he had crawled into last night. In this time just before sunset, he always felt snug, safe, and contented among his kind.

Soldiers walked by on their perimeter route. Radic could just make out the low grumbles of one of them complaining about new shift rotas. It brought back fond memories of

Radic's own homeland security days, that innocent time before they sent you out into the real thick of it. Now here he was, over the hill at 190 days old by human time. He had a good maybe 100 days left before his visits to the hospital became fairly regular. Well, at least Gradulk would be there with him at the end.

A weak but persistent headache throbbed behind his eyes. In front of him, a woman prattled on about her upcoming fungi show; how all the posh were coming, how it was in aid of the Duke House orphans who had been born after all their parents were gassed to death, blah, blah, blah... Arrayed behind her was her prized collection of fungi, immaculately groomed. An army of doddering gardeners — no doubt tapped from retirement for the occasion — constantly sprayed the fungi with fine mists as they spoke. Her name was Trepimia, married to the current Windsor Council Secretary Nadalous, and was a dame if ever there was one. He contemplated, as he watched her sensuous mandibles moving, if he was past having another platoon of children again. It would only be his fourth if he did.

Trepimia laid her hand on his arm and leant towards him conspiratorially. "And did you know that our cousins, the termites, actually depend almost entirely on fungi as their prime source of food?"

"No, really, I didn't know that, please continue," Radic said politely.

He did of course know and watched her again without listening to a word. It never hurt to make your subject feel good about themselves during the interview. The termites were damn hippy vegetarian rural folk who constructed great architectural monuments as homes, and lived way too slow for the likes of a city-grown boy like him. They were not cousins either; they were the closest species relative they had.

He took the time as she blathered on, to breathe deep from all his spiracles and really smell this gorgeous woman. There was just the faintest hint of her delicious sexual pheromones; no doubt 'er and ol' hubby were going for a new platoon last night. Though they hadn't succeeded. That too he could smell, or rather smell the absence of. He felt her hand move abruptly off his arm.

"Mr. Radic! If you can't behave, I'll find a reporter who can!" Trepimia whisper-shouted at him, and looked pointedly down at his body.

Damn! It was his spiracles of course she was referring to. He had been caught taking a good whiff of her and that was decidedly not the most polite thing to be doing. He thought he was being subtle about it. "So sorry Mrs. Trepimia, I was thinking of my wife," he lied. "Please continue," and after a slight sniff she continued and he dutifully listened, sort of.

Radic squeezed through the air-vent to the lobby of Diner Ten. He would eat alone tonight. Gradulk had dropped by the office during lunch, all excited about a new nurse he had met and was taking somewhere special tonight. The line was shorter than usual, and Radic noticed with ambivalence that particular soldier was not there. He didn't have to wait for very long before he was scurrying down to the pots in the sink.

The hors d'oeuvre was a rare one and his personal favourite of Diner Ten; a relish of tsunga, chopped and fried with oil, onions, tomatoes, herbs and spices, and given a huge dollop of peanut butter near the end. Radic spent a full minute savouring its full flavours.

Mindful of yesterday's brash performance, he cautiously looked around before moving on. That's when he noticed the warming drawer was slightly open, which could mean possibly… a whole plate of real relish! Carefully, he made his way down to the floor and crept along the wall to the edge of the stove. Many diners had gone before him here tonight, he could smell, and then a heady waft of what was surely exactly what he had initially hoped for.

Once inside the warmer, he saw he was correct, a plate loaded like a mountain with relish and Sadza, a truly dribble-icious, stiff maize-meal porridge. Nor was he alone, he counted ten others quietly munching away at the feast. It wasn't a problem; their whole local colony combined would have trouble finishing it off before dawn. Radic made his way onto the plate and settled in a free space on top the relish. Breathing deep of the phenomenal scent that filled the air around him like a warm blanket, he took a moment to appreciate and savour its subtleties.

Light leapt through the warming drawer's thin gap and blazed in a ribbon along the black grimy floor. Radic froze, they all did. Several times a shadow blotted out the light, and Radic nearly crapped himself out of fear, and then did. The human must want the meal, it was going to open the drawer any second now, and find them all standing like idiots drooling on it.

However, the human didn't open the drawer and the light stayed on. Radic heard nothing of the usual noises either. No, things were being moved, drawers and cupboards opened, the rattle of pots and plates, the jingle of cutlery; as if the human was making a meal. Strange though as here they were sitting on a whole one. The other diners stirred, some carried on eating, others were caught between eating and fleeing. Radic was just damn curious. It was strategically advisable to stay where they were while the light remained on; statistics ruled in favour of this inaction. Radic nonetheless had to see what was going on. The furore of sound was now certainly beyond that of just a meal.

The angled band of light, its heat a warm caress, stroked over his body as he passed through it. The noise outside had lessened, so he hurried up the open side and peeked out over the edge, blinking rapidly to adjust to the awful brightness.

The kitchen looked chaotic, all the cupboards and draws open but bare. A human launched into view from outside the diner, the low risk one. He went over to the windows and closed them, at this Radic felt his stomach grow cold. There was no high breeze tonight, nor was there anything cooking on the stove. Two actions that in the past had been noted to cause the windows to be closed, there was also a third action.

Radic's breath became shallow and weak, he could barely hold on to the edge of the warmer draw, even with his hard limb spikes carefully positioned. The human turned away from the window and crouched to peer inside the cupboard underneath the sink. Radic, with every vestige of his willpower bundled up and rammed into his limbs, sprinted along the warmer draw edge and leapt for the wall.

Radic missed it by millimetres, even when he opened his wings right at the end, and fell into a huge open plastic bag holding hundreds of other smaller plastic bags. By the time he had fought his way up and out of the polyurethane nightmare, he saw the human far above him. Taping shut the air-vents he had been headed for.

There was only one avenue of escape left, out the kitchen door. Radic leapt from the bag, opened his wings wide and flew. He made it around the cooker and was just getting to the door, flush against the cooker, when the human zipped by and pulled the door halfway closed. Radic, with all engines ago, caught in the door's slip stream, slammed head first into the door's side, bounced, and plummeted to the floor barely conscious.

Radic was caught in a fog of pain and the brightly coloured explosions of a concussion. His limbs were wholly unresponsive, and he could just make out the human crouched down in the centre of the kitchen floor. It held a can bearing bright bands of red and yellow, and if Radic wasn't mistaken a picture of his kind featured large amongst others. The human began to read the very small inscriptions on the can's side, there was a lot of them, and hope began to kindle in Radic's addled mind. Again marshalling all his might, he urged his limbs to move and tried to shake his head to clear it as well. Three legs twitched and his head feebly flopped to one side.

The human stood and aimed the can towards the kitchen counter. The can's end erupted in a plume of white gas that jetted to the counter and rolled over it. Abruptly it stopped and the human read the can's inscriptions once more.

Radic tried again one last time to move, and something clicked deep inside. In an instant he was on his feet again and shook his head vigorously. The explosions in his mind ceased, and the horizon settled into something level. The door opening was half a metre away, the human was now crouching again.

Radic ran.

The human placed the can on the floor and once more set it going; he quickly turned and jumped away into the corridor, closing the door mid-leap with one trailing hand.

Radic spied the door close in slow motion, he was aware of the human far above him and then a sharp pain, as his head once more slammed into the door. Radic dropped like a stone, and idly almost in a dream-state observed a green towel being stuffed under the slight gap between the door and floor.

Diner Ten's safety rating had just dropped to zero. Zero days since last catastrophic occurrence. Zero survivors is what catastrophic meant, all souls lost in Diner Ten. Radic thought about turning his head to see his oncoming doom, but he could picture the rolling clouds like massive storm fronts gathering above near the ceiling. Soon they would roll on down in great whirling soft white billows, and just their advancing invisible legions would smite him dead.

In the short time left, Radic did not blame or curse the human for his impending death; this was just the way of things. He should have noticed how few diners there were in the usually popular Diner Ten, should have taken note; his kind had a sixth sense about these things. Perhaps he had known and ignored it, whatever it was it was all moot now. His time had come to an end; at least now he would get to see if there was anything after this life, though he had never thought there would be, and still didn't.

The can sang Radic's last lullaby, its voice hoarse and reedy just like his own had become over the long years. Radic thought then of his progeny out and about in the world. He had fathered ninety children, seventy had survived their first five days, forty five their military conscriptions, and last count was thirty nine. Most of them had already brought three or more platoons of their own into the world. So he could consider himself as grandfather to at least one thousand seven hundred grandchildren. It was below average but still enough to be proud of.

Have I taught my children any better than I was taught, Radic questioned, and it was his last conscious query. His limbs started to twitch and contort as though trying to rip themselves off and crawl away. Radic turned his head and looked upwards, just in time to see the thick cloud race across the short distance that remained. The legions hit his brain next and everything just clicked off, leaving only a fading static after-image of the advancing cloud and a last note of the screaming lullaby, softly echoing down to nothing at all.

Ivor Hartmann is a Zimbabwean writer, and author of *Mr. Goop* (Vivlia, 2010). He was nominated for the UMA Award ('Earth Rise', 2009), awarded The Golden Baobab Prize ('Mr. Goop', 2009), and a finalist for The Yvonne Vera Award ('A Mouse amongst Men' 2011). His writing has appeared in *African Writing Magazine, Wordsetc, Munyori Literary Journal, Something Wicked*, and *The Apex Book of World SF 2*, among others. He is the co-editor/publisher of the *African Roar* annual anthology, and on the advisory board of Writers International Network Zimbabwe.

Chanting Shadows

Mbonisi P. Ncube

A boy entered the field of maize stalks like a darting arrow. The men, chopping at brown stalks in preparation for the planting season, looked up at him with startled gazes. On his face was written a look of fear that the boy quickly passed to the other men. Mzala Joe, the oldest of the farm workers put his hand on the boy's shoulder. He always spoke first in such matters. He was sixty-one and knew a lot about life.

"How many, Jonasi?" Mzala Joe asked the boy calmly, his brow rising slightly.

Jonasi remained silent and perturbed.

Mzala Joe shook him firmly again, "How many, mfana?"

Jonasi wiped his sweaty face with his hands. He looked at Mzala Joe with an expression of anguish and then he spoke with a clattering voice like cutlery falling to a concrete slab. "Hundred... or so, Mzala..."

A fire of questions followed his answer. The men clamoured and gathered around them, all wanting to know what was going on. A baby, on the far side of the field, began crying.

"Will someone make that baby stop?" Mzala Joe shouted, his voice ringing with an unusual metal-grinding rasp. A hush fell at once. Mzala Joe put his hand on Jonasi again. "Were there... were there any youths among them?"

In the past months, the word *youth* had metamorphosed to mean sheer terror.

Jonasi remained silent, only studying the ground below his feet. Then he slowly nodded, as his answer came in short gasps, "Most... most that I saw were youths... sixteen to twenty-one maybe... never in the war themselves. They must be from the training camps. They all were wearing army regalia, and were carrying whips, machetes, rocks, axes, and knives..."

162

Mzala Joe nibbled at his lower lip as a commotion ensued.

A man cried out in anger, "Are we to suffer at the hands of these born-free virgins... these children who still have traces of their mother's breast milk on their lips?"

"Today they will meet their match!" another shouted.

"Not on this land, never!" chanted one, stamping the ground vigorously.

They retreated to pick up their tools.

Mzala Joe smiled at the furore. "Relax men! Men, relax!" he called out to them, his voice rising amidst the exclamations and his raised hand waving in the afternoon air. Addressing Jonasi, he asked, "Where are they coming from? We must prepare ourselves mfana."

"From the east, and two of the youths have AK-47s," said Jonasi.

"Guns?" Mzala Joe's voice dithered, and the lines on his face deepened.

Jonasi continued, "They passed through the Bentley Farm yesterday and I hear they did good damage. McNamara has been trying to contact Bentley but the telephone is dead. For all we know, they could be dead."

"Dead?" a man whispered to another.

The baby began crying again, and Mzala Joe became quiet as its cries undulated in the silence.

"Kondozi is our refuge," he finally began, "And strong must be the man who protects his house or land." A handful of men uttered incoherent answers.

"We must fight," Mzala Joe repeated, desperately wanting to capture the men to his favour. Unrelenting, he looked at Jonasi, who had become quite calm in the blossoming furore. Then he raised his hands, and a dead silence descended.

"How many minutes before they reach the gate of Kondozi Farm?" Mzala Joe asked.

"Does McNamara know?" said another man.

"Guns... does McNamara have them?"

163

"One question at a time, madoda!" Mzala Joe shouted. "Jonasi will answer all your questions. Please, Jonasi?"

Jonasi stared at Mzala Joe, an emptiness gleaming in his eyes. "McNamara sent me here to warn you. They are coming madoda..."

"McNamara, he has guns doesn't he?" Mzala Joe asked. "You work in their house. You should know mfana."

Jonasi shook his head.

Mzala became quiet as his eyes locked with the other men's, who wavered with lurid fear, and he knew they wanted him to say something they wanted to hear. In such situations, a man must be careful not to dampen other men's spirits. Neither must he lead them into obvious oblivion. Mzala looked at the men again, feeling a surge of strength sweep over his body like a voltage shot. It was a feeling of authority, like he was a film action hero, or an important chief in a village indaba.

Joe was the oldest inhabitant of Kondozi Farm, having arrived at fifteen years old still bound by the first chains of adolescence. Then the country had been full of landmines, bloody battles, and ravished by an insane war between white and black men. He had run away from the 'call up' when it had come to his village. This would be the same call up that would claim his four brothers and leave them buried somewhere in the jungles of Chimoio in Mozambique. He never forgave himself for not running away with them to the Liberation War. He wondered whether they had forgiven him for not joining them on their patriotic quest.

McNamara usually joked that he had groomed the boy. And it was true. He would joke and tell others how, late one stormy December night, Mzala Joe had turned up at his farmhouse doorstep, begging for a meal and a place to shelter from the pounding rain. Out of pity, McNamara had given Mzala Joe a job of feeding the chickens. Mzala Joe had worked well, treated every worker like they were part of his family, and McNamara had seen all of this. In those days there was a word that the farm workers addressed each other with. To him they said Baas, which he did not like, but between themselves as a show of equality or respect, they used mzala, which meant 'good friend'. He called Joe 'mzala' the next day. And that name stuck for good.

Jonasi looked at Mzala Joe's greying head then at the sun, which had hidden its face amongst grey clouds. A look of concern was on Mzala Joe's face.

"McNamara has guns. He is well armed," Jonasi said.

"That is good news," Mzala Joe said, nodding his head. He squinted at the sun, wishing it could become dark. "We must prepare," he added.

Minutes passed. Very long minutes. Mzala Joe raised his hand at the men, but spoke to the women at the far end of the field first; women were always the first casualties of war. "You must go now. Take the children with you, find somewhere safe to hide. The battle has begun. We must now fight!"

The men looked at Jonasi, fear their only countenance.

"White people are known for preparing well..." a man's voice rose in the tumult.

"Yes! He will know what to do!" More men uttered in unison and Mzala Joe looked at the sky again, choosing to ignore the chaos. A clever man, whether white or black, prepares well, he told himself.

Up in the sky, Mzala Joe saw the birds gliding freely. He wished he was one of them. "How long have these invasions been going on?" he asked Jonasi rhetorically. They had discussed it, McNamara and he, the day before, this issue of land invasions. There was disorder to the whole program, with only few people making money out of it. He remembered what McNamara had said: "They say a man without his land grows like a seedless plant, ready to wither and leave no family line. A man must fight for his land. I'm white but I belong here too. I know no other land except this farm. Generations of my family have toiled for this farm to be what it is now. Why then must I not fight for what my family has built? For what is mine?"

Jonasi cut short Mzala Joe's remembrance. "The Bentleys, they were the sixth to be attacked this week. Kondozi is the next..."

"In seven days?" Mzala Joe looked startled. He cast a long worried glance at Jonasi, who nodded at nothing. "They could be breaking down our gate by now..."

"Mzala Joe, do you think that I am superior?"

Mzala Joe removed the stem of grass between his teeth. With it, he drew a circle on the dusty ground, before stealing a glance at McNamara's blue eyes.

"Am I superior, Mzala Joe, because my skin is white?"

Mzala Joe did not answer then. He remained quiet, his mind distant but his answer near.

"Yes and no," Mzala Joe said after a while.

"I do not understand..." McNamara said, his eyes unblinking.

Mzala Joe stared aimlessly at the billowing smoke from the farmhouse. "Yes, as my boss. And no, because you have a white skin does not mean you are superior."

McNamara remained quiet, a tint of life showing in his sullen eyes. "In my life, I have never considered the colour of my skin being superior to anyone else's. We are just people, my old friend. Just people. None is superior. None has the right to kill anyone. We are all born the same way. We all die the same way."

Mzala Joe nodded. "That is how I see the world. I think all men are created equal," he said. "That is God's plan."

When it happened, it happened fast.

The first shot splintered the afternoon air, breaking the silence. The men, surprised by the sudden thundering, all scurried in cowering fear. Some dived for cover, hitting the brown earth with their bare sweating bodies. Only Mzala Joe remained upright, like some sort of demigod, seemingly not fazed at all. He dashed to one end of the field waving his arms in the air. He stopped then, to curse, glaring at the sky. Again, he ran to the other end, and began to spit on the ground. The other men looked on in fear. Something was wrong with Mzala Joe. He would never act like this, not unless he was angry.

And he was angry.

The second shot took them all by surprise. It thundered like a monster dismissed from hell. There was an abrupt silence. Smoke billowed from McNamara's farmhouse. The men cowered, crawled, shouted, and shrieked, like trapped mice in a gutter.

There was another shot, and another, and another...

McNamara looked at the dead log that he and Mzala Joe were sitting on. "Quite funny," he began. "To think that this log we're sitting on once thrived with potent life and was green and had succulent leaves. To think it used to produce fruit every year-".

"Funny?" Mzala Joe cut in. He shook his aged head. "I do not understand."

"Look at it this way, my old friend," McNamara said. "This tree here, it has grown on this ground for decades. It is good that it died here on the land it was born."

Though Mzala Joe nodded in approval, he still did not understand fully.

McNamara continued, "Jonasi, the family cook."

Mzala Joe nodded. Confusion was all over his face. "Why do you mention him? Is anything wrong?"

"He's fine. I sent him on an errand, over to Maywood farm yesterday. They were not there. They just disappeared, even the farm workers. He found new people living on the farm."

Mzala Joe picked up some soil on the ground, and began to rub it with his hands. "Could it have been the invasions?" he asked the question whose answer he did not want to hear.

McNamara did not answer right away.

"It has begun, Joe," he said after a while.

Mzala Joe looked away, and McNamara saw that the old man was in deep thought. He knew that if there was a man in the farm who would fight with his life for Kondozi, that man would have to be Mzala Joe. But right now, McNamara could see that Mzala Joe was troubled. Never had he seen him like this. He had grown to love and trust this old man. Beneath those lines of Mzala Joe's face lay wisdom.

Mzala Joe picked a stem of grass, unaware of the colossal respect McNamara had for him. He chewed almost impetuously.

"Is it going to end?" McNamara asked, his eyes fixed on Mzala Joe's face. Mzala Joe did not reply. McNamara looked at his land, his farm that was on the verge of destruction. Secretly, he wished he could say a prayer with Mzala. He looked at him and asked.

"Mzala Joe, do you think that I'm superior?"

Five clear shots thundered, and an angry arm of black thick smoke choked and twirled in the sky. Orange flames leapt and licked around where the farmhouse was situated. Mzala Joe's face was painted with crude bewilderment.

And just then, they heard them coming.

At first it was the sound of their voices, a surmounting angry mob of voices, screaming, bellowing, chanting, and getting closer.

"They are coming madoda!" Jonasi's terrified voice rose in the furore of incoming danger. He suddenly made a run for it, and then stopped. "What do we do, Mzala Joe?" There was fear in the tone of his words.

"Be calm young man," Mzala voice reassured. He looked at the curling hand of smoke.

"I cannot... cannot, die for something useless as land."
Jonasi's gesturing hands shook in the air. He finally
dropped to the ground, overcome by fear.

Mzala Joe approached the cowering boy, unchallenged by
the nearing chants. He picked up an axe with his other hand
and glared angrily in the direction the noise was coming
from.

Mzala Joe whistled sharply, calling all the men to gather
around him.

*"I think all men are created equal. That is God's plan,"
Mzala Joe said.*

*McNamara also picked a blade of grass. "So, like this
log, you prefer to live your life in the land where you were
born?"*

*Mzala Joe hesitated. His reply, when it finally came,
snapped like the string of a new guitar. "Yes."*

*McNamara looked at him, smiling, "Now tell me, to what
extent would you go to defend what you believe in?"*

*"To the very death of me, if it needs be," Mzala Joe
answered.*

The toyi-toying group appeared like a myriad of killer bees
on an attack run. They were chanting and singing in
powerful unison. Each second they inched closer to their
prey, their assortment of protruding tools, axes, huge
culling knives, knobkerries, sticks, and stones, shining in
their hands. They had come with one intention. It was
written on their faces, and clear in their chanting.

Mzala Joe and his farm workers did not flinch. But hearts
were waning. No men can run away from the clutches of
terror. Terror is sticky, and it glues a man to his weakness,
bones and flesh.

Mzala Joe stood in front, steadfast, and defiant. A
machete and axe gleamed in his hands. "We will not move
an inch!" he shouted and looked at the sky. The sun had
disappeared, and cold clouds rolled above, as if they were

waiting for the drama to unfold. The sun had decided not to watch this fight.

"I said we will not be provoked to move!" Mzala Joe screamed at the top of his bracing lungs. He felt the strange energy of passion wrap itself over him like a blanket. It gave him strength and he hoped it would not abandon him when he needed it most.

The breaths of men behind him stung his neck. Breaths full of fear, he could tell. He felt abandoned, alone amongst the men who were rallying behind him. Droplets of cold sweat inundated his face, and his muscles stung his nerves. He tightened his grip on his two weapons.

By now, the invaders were quite near, with some haphazardly crashing through the maize field. One of them set heaps of stalks on fire. Black smoke danced in the air. Still, Mzala Joe and the field of men behind him remained adamant. The strange energy was still with him. It only began to waver as he saw one of them waving in the air on a long stick, the orange shirt he knew so well.

"You are serious, Mzala?" pressed McNamara.

"I have fought all my life. Fought poverty, fought for my dead brothers' blood, fought to where I am today. I can still fight for what I believe in." A raw, palatable passion was in Mzala Joe's voice as he said this.

McNamara nodded, and then he stood up and tucked in his favourite orange shirt. He put his hand on Mzala Joe's shoulder. The red sky was beginning to darken. "I can still fight also," he said. "I will be honoured to fight with you, my brother."

The orange shirt was soiled with fresh blood. It flapped freely in the air, as if it was a gruesome war flag. The mass of people encroached dangerously. They were clearly audible now, and their confused chanting flooded the atmosphere to the brim. They stopped about twenty metres from Mzala Joe's group. For a while they remained there, their faces sweating.

Then they bolted towards the farm workers.

Mzala Joe and the men behind him remained where they were, their hearts pounding like iron gongs. The furious group stopped midway. They stood there, fierce and furious.

"Pamberi neLand Reform!" yelled the leader to his followers, who took up his chant immediately, and with effortless enthusiasm. "Our forefathers *fought* for this land, our ancestors *toiled* for it, and *died* for it... and yet, yet these white men here, all of them, they still control us! They still run the country. They still make us feel inferior in our own territory. We are stopping this today. Kondozi is ours, and no white farmer will rule us from now on!" He shook his fist into the air, and then turned to glare at the women and men behind him. "Listen to me comrades; we are taking everything that is rightfully ours! Down with Boer! Pamberi neLand Reform!" He shouted again, stamping on the ground, brandishing his AK-47. The mob reacted passionately, and the women ululated, dust swirling from the ground.

"We will burn it, burn all this down! Burn the white men and you, all his workers! Burn everything that opposes us!" he said, paused, and stared at Mzala Joe. "Down with sell-outs!"

"Down with them!" the mob reverberated, weapons dancing in the still air.

Mzala stood his ground, his mind reeling away from the moment for a few seconds. He knew how hard it had been for him to grow up without a home, without a history. The war had destroyed it all, along with the memory of his parents. The 'chaff' had to be washed away by the rain, the soldiers had mocked. And Mzala had not known the meaning of the sentence then. It had been a hard time, but war was war, and he could not live in the past. He remembered the darkness of the jungle, the howling, pelting rain, and the beasts that rustled the leaves of the forest as he and his brothers had run for their lives; running away from the soldiers who had killed their parents just for speaking a different language. And in the midst of that run, his lungs almost giving in, he had sworn to fight for what was his. One day would come back, and he would fight this cowardice. He would never make the mistake of running away ever again. But like this man in front of him now, he would fight for what he believed in. He had only been a boy then, but he wished he had fought for his mother's house, instead of having to watch it burn away into the night. He had never fixed that guilt in his life. And every day, the hole grew in his heart, an emptiness staring at him, coaxing him to fill it up. This was his home now, and he would not lose it again.

They were rounding up the horses in the barn when McNamara came up to him and asked, "Mzala, do you support what the men are doing, going around, invading farms and taking over?"

Mzala looked at him, his hand imperceptibly on his chin. "Every man needs a home once it has been taken away from him. These men believe they are correcting that. You know in your hearts of hearts that the white people did us wrong, they colonised us, and took over what was ours..."

"That has never left my mind, Mzala," McNamara interjected. "But we are the same people now."

"We can never be the same, sir," Mzala replied, staring hard at the man. "We are good friends, but we have never been the same."

"So do you believe that what they are doing is warranted?" McNamara pressed on.

Mzala went quiet. "They believe it is their right to take what is theirs. No man must lose his home. The lion protects his territory, and if it taken away from him, he might limp away, but soon he returns to fight for it and claim it for his own."

McNamara nodded silently.

"Pamberi!" the man shouted again, and as he did so, he dropped the orange shirt on the ground between the two groups.

Jonasi broke out wailing. "The shirt, Mzala Joe! They've killed McNamara. They've murdered all of them!"

The leader of the group laughed. "Sell-outs!" he hissed, spitting on the ground. The women behind him cheered, and one moved in front of the leader, gyrating in the dust with youthful enthusiasm.

Then, Mzala suddenly darted forward, like a poisoned arrow chasing an enraged buffalo, towards the man in front of him. He saw it all clearly now; the soldiers, their macabre bayonets sinking into the flesh of his mother's body; the sound of her piercing scream as the steel gored into her flesh; the hungry, lapping flames, devouring up the thatched roof of their home; his trembling heart as he ran away from the scene, a fist of revenge curling up his chest. He would not be running away again. Not today. *Never...*

Two obliterating shots pierced the air. Mzala Joe felt the strange energy leave him at once. He heard the raucous laugh of the soldiers in the distance once again, the screams of his begging mother, and then a ringing voice filled his ears. Like a rag doll, he jerked backwards, as the unseen force of the bullets pierced his flesh. For a while he stood as if nothing had happened, with his mouth agape, dazed. He suddenly felt an exhilarating lightness cover him, and smiling, he saw his mother extending her arm to him. Like a heavy sack, he slowly slumped, his cheek hitting the dry ground with a painful thud. From the blurred vision, he last saw them, the men and the women, now blurred shadows, still chanting and chanting, and then his eyes rolled carelessly as an acute darkness overwhelmed him.

Afterwards, Jonasi covered the body with the orange shirt.

Master and servant, some workers said. But some said they wanted to think of the two as good friends. Good friends who had been loyal to each other. Good friends who had dared overcome the colour of their skins, and the tone of their languages, and above all, good friends who had fought for their land and died for it.

Above, as the two groups stood silently demarcated by the body of Mzala Joe with their weapons and tools cast on the silent ground, was a deafening roar of thunder. Thick falling torrents suddenly pelted the dry ground. Another farming season had begun.

And the rain would wash away the blood...

Mbonisi P. Ncube is a 28-year- old Zimbabwean currently residing in South Africa where he works for an engineering firm as Design Technician. He has been writing for more than six years and his work has been published in *StoryTime*, *Munyori Literary Journal*, *Ibhuku*, among others. His poem 'The Way' was featured in a UK anthology of rhyming poems *A Time to Rhyme*. 'Chanting Shadows' was awarded the 2011 Yvonne Vera Award. Two of his crime novels *The Munhumutapa Candidate* and *The Nocturnal life of Mrs Smith* were short-listed the 2011 Citizen Book Prize. He is currently working on a poetry collection.

Snake of the Niger Delta

Chimdindu Mazi-Njoku

They call me the Snake. You see, I had a difficult childhood, but I've almost always demonstrated an uncanny gift of coming out of seemingly hopeless situations. They say I am slippery, maybe I am. This is my story.

I was only ten when my father first took my mother and me along with him to Abuja to buy the goods he sold. I guess my father must have come across a huge windfall and decided to use that opportunity to show us the roads without potholes he had always told us about. Once I had asked my father why he always held my mother close to him, especially when she had only her wrapper tied over her breasts, and stroked her slender arms repeatedly. He had said to me, "Because her skin is black and smooth, just like the roads in the North". I remember being jealous. My mother found it difficult to believe that such roads existed in Nigeria, and so did I. Not because of how the roads were in my village — there were none worthy of being called roads. We disbelieved because the few times we visited Port Harcourt, the rickety buses we travelled in often hobbled like a child learning how to walk, rolling in and out of mini craters. Port Harcourt was the biggest, most urbanised city I had ever travelled to before then and there were many potholes there. How then could there be a place without potholes on their roads, I wondered.

When we made the trip and I saw that it was true, my young mind wondered why this place that we had spent countless hours travelling to was so developed while my village looked eerily backward. I didn't see things we had in my village; like the numerous gas flares that made everywhere searing hot and especially made hairy people smell like roasted goats; the networks of pipes that made so much noise that I couldn't hear myself talk in my dreams;

the soil that was drenched with crude oil which made it soggy and barren; the oil workers decked in orange coveralls with striped, cowry-shaped logos who came by boats to work in my village — probably because of the lack of good roads. Father told me that part of the money used to build all the nice roads in Abuja came from my village. I found it hard to believe that my village was that rich.

Four days after we arrived in Abuja we began our journey back home. I was tired and dreaded the long distance so I went to sleep shortly after we left the scenic capital city. There are only two things I can remember now: that we travelled in a station wagon, and the screams...

I woke up to see aunt Ngozi, my mother's cousin, holding my hands in a large room with a bare cement floor containing little apart from eight flea-infested beds and six comatose fans. The mattresses were so thin they made me wonder whether they were meant to be slept on or used as blankets to keep the obese mosquitoes away. A few light bulbs were suspended from the peeling ceiling that boasted an impressive network of antique cobwebs.

I was in a hospital.

I would later learn that the car had somersaulted five times and slammed into a tree, after my father ran the car into a small but deep pothole, in a bid to avoid a larger one. The depth of the killer pothole had gone unnoticed as it was filled with muddy rain water. I was the only survivor and it was a miracle; considering that I was pulled out of the twisted wreck of metal completely unhurt. Right then, I knew my parents were dead because repairs had not come in time, if ever, to a stretch of federal road somewhere in Delta State.

Poor relatives are distant relatives, so my mother's people abandoned me. They had never cared anyway so it made no difference. They were far better off financially than we were, but my mother became a pariah to her family when she married my poor father against their vehement refusal. She was Igbo, from Anambra State, while he was a poor man of Rivers stock. I was taken in by my father's only surviving brother. He was a dirt-poor, lame, childless widower, so I practically had to fend for myself.

I would later survive a pipeline explosion that killed twelve people and maimed dozens more, a severe bout of diarrhoea caught from a local epidemic, and cerebral malaria. I have literally slipped out of the cold hands of death unscathed a good number of times. However, that is not why they call me the Snake.

The primary school in my village wasn't well attended. It wasn't because we were not interested in education, no. Parts of the ancient zinc roof that covered the classrooms in parts had caved in, and leaked badly; since it rained most of the year, this was a major hindrance to our learning. All we did most times was play and pluck fruits from the weary trees in the school compound. Our teachers did not show up every day. Whenever they did the lessons were taught without enthusiasm. The teachers used to tell us, with scowls on their faces, that if we wanted to learn, we should tell the government to pay them their salaries. I always felt sorry for them, for they were often owed up to six months of salaries and consequently had a near-permanent peckish look shrouding their forlorn faces.

During one English class our teacher asked, "Can any of you give me an example of what goes up and never comes down?"

We all believed we had the answer because all our hands shot up, and we screamed out "Uncle, uncle I know it… me, uncle… I can answer, uncle!" He eyed the class and picked me to answer. Of course, I knew, like most of my classmates did, that the most obvious answer was age, but I had a different opinion.

"The fire that burns from the big standing pipes," I said. I hadn't known then that 'gas flares' would have been more appropriate. Well, everyone burst into laughter, not because I didn't use the right words, but because they felt I had gotten the answer woefully wrong.

"Why are you all laughing?" the teacher barked, his eyes menacing like that of our policemen when they are intimidating a bus driver who refused to 'roger' them. He went on, "Do you know that those flames you see, they are called gas flares by the way, have been burning for over thirty years? Don't laugh at him; he is right for saying that!"

Silence enveloped the class. I was happy to have been vindicated and I looked around, sneering at my classmates. Having gained the full attention of the class, the teacher went on, "Do you know that every second these flames are alight, millions upon millions of naira are going into the pockets of our corrupt rulers? Yet we are owed salaries; our tiny salaries! Look at your desks, made of rubbish wood! Our roof has been leaking for years and the government does not care. I have to write on the wall with the chalk because there are no blackboards; simple blackboards! No library, no books, no laboratories, not even one typewriter, not to talk of a computer. Well, where is the electricity to power the computer? None! No fans in your classrooms, there are holes on the floor, cracks on the walls... What a pity!"

His eyes were now crimson red. Blinking away tears, he finally said, "Please my dear children, we don't have leaders that are concerned about us in this country; we are on our own. I won't lie to you. If you think you are getting education here, you are deceiving yourselves. I advise you to read for your own good and develop your minds. Read everything you see; newspapers, books, magazines, always read! You will become more intelligent by doing so and it will make your future brighter. A doctor cannot save lives with his bare hands."

He wiped a tear from his eye with his thumb, took his notes, and left the class in a hurry. His words still echo in my head — "always read".

A crude-oil production site was situated close to my late uncle's home and there too a camp for the workers. It was closer to the creek than my primary school. Since the bulk of my chores consisted of water — fetching it, washing, fishing sometimes — I spent a good part of each day at the creek. It was our only source of water and we did everything with it including drinking and cooking. Most times I joined my friends to bath, defecate, swim and play 'touch-the-river-bed.' We did all this in the same stretch of water albeit at different sections.

I started hanging around the rig camp; staring in awe at the huge machines, generators, rigs, the constant flurry of activity, and the people that worked there. I wished to go in there so I could boast about it to my friends.

I got lucky one day.

While sitting outside the camp on the plastic bucket I used to carry on my head from the distant creek, one tall, well-built young man dressed in grease-stained coveralls saw me. He was walking back into the camp with a nylon bag full of guavas gripped firmly in his hand. His wide smile and shiny teeth made me feel at ease immediately. He laid his hand on my dandruff-infested head and said to me, "Young man, I always see you here. Do you want to come inside the camp?"

"Yes uncle," I answered, looking up at him with pleading eyes.

"Oya, let's go in ore mi," he said. I was overjoyed! I finally would have bragging rights, I thought.

In those days there wasn't a battalion of soldiers guarding the oil companies' on-shore production sites. It was just two or three security men. He later told me he was Yoruba, and 'ore mi' meant 'my friend.' I started calling him uncle Oremi and he didn't mind, even though it always made him and his colleagues laugh.

I had just turned twelve then and I was small for my age. Uncle Oremi always made sure I ate to my satisfaction whenever I came to see him; and I tried to go everyday. The living-quarters in the camp were beautiful and the air inside the buildings was clean, cool, and crisp, because of the air conditioning.

Uncle Oremi had a good collection of books, magazines, and engineering journals, which he always brought with him, and I devoured them all. I read newspapers too whenever I saw them. He was so pleased that I loved to read. He brought me textbooks, short story collections, novels, an English dictionary, and even an encyclopaedia. Months later we could talk about a wide variety of issues; my mental age had now far surpassed my chronological age. He said I was a bright and clever kid. The combination of nutritious food, clean drinking water, and a voracious appetite for eclectic knowledge, made me grow bigger, stronger, more handsome, and more knowledgeable. My teacher had been right; my self-confidence soared.

One day, uncle Oremi was escorting me back home and we were halfway to the gate when the big boss, a Scottish man named Mr. Robert, beckoned him. I followed out of curiosity for there were several workers attending to a metal contraption that rose about five feet into the air, with metal limbs sticking out of it on both sides like a fir tree viewed in two dimensions. The image was familiar to me.

"What's wrong with it?" I asked Mr. Robert. We had never really talked apart from the waves, thumbs-up, and greetings, we exchanged occasionally whenever I came to see uncle Oremi.

"Do you know what that is?" he asked me.

"Yes. It's called a Christmas-tree," I answered, smiling.

A look of surprise, no, shock cascaded down his face. He looked at me, turned to look at uncle Oremi, then back to me and asked, "Son, how do you know that?"

"I have read about it in engineering journals," I replied, still smiling.

That was how I found myself in British International School in Port Harcourt. Uncle Oremi later told me that Mr. Robert — who was childless having lost his teenage daughter to leukaemia — was so impressed that he paid for my six years of secondary education in the rarefied, exclusive learning centre. The contrast was alarming! The school was like heaven compared to the dilapidated, derelict block of three rooms that constituted my village primary school. I later saw that the Federal Government schools were generally better catered to than the State Government schools. Also, the schools in the townships like Port Harcourt were better maintained than those in remote villages like mine. The inequality was glaring.

I was initially snubbed by my new school mates, who mostly came from upper middle-class homes. However, I earned their respect when it became clear that my intelligence was superior to theirs, and I was quite proud of where I came from. I stayed with uncle Oremi at his place in Port Harcourt during school holidays and he took good care of me.

One defining moment of my life came one morning when I opened my soap-dish to take a bath and it suddenly dawned on me that I had never washed the soap dish since I got it, yet I took soap out of it at least once a day to wash my body. Even though the soap dish was inanimate and could have no feelings, it didn't stop me from feeling selfish. The soap dish must have felt so cheated! The significance of the whole thing was the irony. The irony was disturbing, and more so when I realised that it characterised what was happening to my village and most other oil-producing communities in the Niger Delta. I was the politician, the soap was the crude oil and my village was the soap dish. Soap in a dirty soap dish... poverty in the midst of stupendous wealth. I washed the soap dish immediately, and every day after that. I took up a cause that day to do all I could to correct the injustices being done to my people.

I always came out top in my class and by the end of the six years, I was second best overall; the best student was a pretty Indian girl I had had a huge crush on. My academic excellence qualified me for a full scholarship at one of three top universities in the UK. I chose Oxford University. Uncle Oremi was so proud of me, and so was Mr. Robert. I can't remember a time when I was happier.

In Oxford I met Tunde, the son of a wealthy politician in Nigeria. His father had just been appointed the overall head of a federal parastatal, after serving as head of projects and maintenance for some years. He used to boast endlessly about it. Being the only son of his father, Tunde always worked with him on everything; from giving out contracts to collecting bribes.

Tunde would have five thousand pounds one day and be broke by the next day. He would often hoodwink contract seekers into giving him large sums of money to influence his father. He had two expensive habits: women and cocaine.

One day Tunde told me that there was a white man in the UK who had just founded a construction company and was seeking a contract to resurface and maintain a stretch of road in the eastern part of Nigeria. The problem, he explained, was that the contract was to be given to his dad's friend, who would then give his dad forty percent of the money awarded for the contract, and then use the rest to sort himself out; whether he did the job or not. Tunde would ask the white man to pay the—non-refundable—bid sum for the contract into his account and then pay bribes in cash afterwards to clinch it. The bottom line was that the white man in question had everything to lose if he fell for it. He wanted me to use my intelligence to 'craft' the deal properly.

How can I indulge in what I've criticised all my life? I wondered. Well, I asked him to get me the company profile of the white man. I went through it and smiled; karma would come knocking on someone's door soon.

I asked Tunde to fetch all the copies of his dad's previous dealings he could get without letting his dad know. I told him I needed them so I could prepare the fake documents we would need for the scam; they needed to look fool proof. He flew into Nigeria and came back to the UK a few days later with a large brown envelope which contained more material than I had hoped for.

Tunde was in a hurry and his impetuousness would be his undoing. I asked him to tell me all about how his dad arranged their shady contracts and collected bribes. Tunde, boisterous as he was, was only happy to do that. On the day we were to go seal the deal, Tunde bought me a fabulous Dolce & Gabbana suit complete with a Pringle of Scotland shirt, Salvatore Ferragamo shoes, silk tie, and glasses. He said I was to pose as the lawyer. I didn't mind.

"Nothing will happen," he said. "My father's aide asked the mugu to deal with me only. Besides, the man will be incriminating himself as a bribe-giver if he's stupid enough to go running to the Metropolitan Police later." But Tunde was wrong. Something would happen.

As we sat in the hotel room Tunde paid for at the Ritz, I asked him to bring out all the fake documents and go over the lies we would be telling the white man. He gleefully did, his eyes still burning too bright from the morning's snort of cocaine. As our expected guest knocked, Tunde rushed to open the door. His face twisted into a contorted mixture of fear and bewilderment when the white man strode into the room with two burly police officers trailing closely behind. The white man walked up to me without breaking a stride. I was now on my feet.

"Nice to see you again, Mr. Robert," I said as we shook hands warmly and then hugged.

"These are the fake documents. I have the records of our conversations in my mobile phone; we can transfer them to your laptop right away," I said as we broke free from the embrace.

Tunde looked at me, shocked witless. I smiled; the kind of mocking smile a defendant's lawyer will give the prosecuting attorney after he wins an acquittal for his clearly guilty client. Tunde was arrested with damning, unimpeachable evidence.

Mr. Robert, who gave me a future against all odds, was the white man Tunde and his father's aide had been planning to dupe.

Tunde's father was the head of the government body in charge of the maintenance of all federal roads in Nigeria: he had been the one responsible for not repairing the bad road that killed my parents.

Revenge, they say, is best served cold. It wasn't just about revenge though, I believe the action I took will save the lives of road users in the future. At least, it would now be difficult to plunder public funds meant for road construction, repair, and maintenance, owing to the massive reforms put in place by the popularity of the case. I was nicknamed the 'Snake' after the Nigerian press started glorifying me for the 'slippery' way I had obtained all the hard evidence used in sending the corrupt politicians to jail. It was okay by me; all I did was translate it into its equivalent in Igbo, my mother's native tongue: Agwo.

You must be wondering why I haven't mentioned my name all through this story. It is no mistake. Forget about my name, just reflect on my story. Remember it... tell it. If you must though, you may call me Agwo: The Snake of the Niger Delta.

Chimdindu Mazi-Njoku was born on April 14, 1985, in Port Harcourt, Rivers State, Nigeria, into a family of six. He is a native of Isuikwato LGA in Abia state, Nigeria. His early childhood years were spent in Port Harcourt where he had his nursery and primary education. He left for Lagos for his secondary education in the prestigious Kings College. In 2001, he was admitted into Federal University of Technology, Owerri, where he majored in Industrial Microbiology. Mazi-Njoku has always been a bibliophile, right from the age of six when he began reading anything and everything that came his way, with a predilection for encyclopaedias and novels. He is an automobile enthusiast, a lover of art, and an advocate of mental emancipation through unbiased, unrelenting enlightenment; literary and otherwise.

Silent Night, Bloody Night

Ayodele Morocco-Clarke

I am standing at the edge of the Lagos Bar Beach where waves roughly beat at my feet. The sea looks stormy and I half turn to catch a glimpse of one of the warning flags; that tiny piece of cloth on a stick, which informs about the temperament of the sea and could be the difference between life and death if heeded. White flags mean 'come on in'; giving a calm, safe and inviting sign for even the not-too-good swimmers. Yellow flags say 'be careful'; indicating that something might be brewing in the belly of the sea. Red flags scream 'Danger! Danger! Keep away'; warning about waters boiling with ferocious waves and strong undercurrents, which could overpower even the strongest of swimmers.

The local folk tell tales about there being a mami-water; a mermaid who lived in the sea and had lost her only daughter. It is said that when the sea was rough, it is because she is angry about not finding her daughter and determined on exacting revenge for the loss of her precious child, she drags unfortunate swimmers into a vortex she creates. On really bad days, the sea at the Bar Beach overflows its banks and floods the roads, which usually lie a good eight hundred metres from the edge of the sea.

Today, red flags are up. I chose a red flag day because I do not want my efforts to be thwarted. I have come to take my life and stand before the sea reflecting on what had been a perfect life until almost two weeks ago.

My name is Ameze Obaze. I was born with what some people refer to as a silver spoon. My father, Osadolor, is a wealthy cocoa merchant and my mother Ivie, a princess from the royal house of Eweka, is a trader who owns many shops and stalls in both the Tejuosho and Balogun markets in Lagos. At just nine days shy of my sixteenth birthday, I

187

am the eldest daughter of their four offspring. Osagie, my brother was born three years before me, and then there are the twins, Iyen and Idehen. Ours was a happy family filled with love and laughter. Mum always had a reason to thank God. She told us over and over again to always count our blessings, and kept saying that she did not know why God singled her out for so many blessings. She had a loving successful husband who made his family his priority, healthy children who were academically gifted, and to add to these, her business was thriving.

We had gone to Benin-City from our Lagos home a few days before Christmas as we did every year. Bini natives from all over the world converged in Benin-City at this time of the year. It was a period I loved and enjoyed as I always caught up with members of my extended family whom I did not get to see otherwise. It was a period of merriment, partying, and unparalleled gossiping.

Mum ensured that we all got new clothes, and everyday different goods—ranging from bags of rice, numerous tubers of yam, bunches of plantain, bags of beans, huge kegs of vegetable oil and palm oil, bags of garri and yam flour; even half a dozen goats and fifty chickens —were delivered to the house. Mum made sure that Efe, the driver, brought home bales of cloth from one of her shops. These cloths were for distribution among the clan women, many of whom made up our extended family and were less privileged than we. Half of the foodstuff was for similar distribution among relatives and friends. The other half was usually cooked during the period we were in Benin-City, with the majority used in feeding the numerous visitors who came to the house to pay social calls on Mum and Dad.

The days whizzed past and before I knew it, Christmas had come and gone. We were supposed to return to Lagos on Saturday the 6th of January 1990. On the Thursday before the return, Osagie, the twins, and I, had gone with our cousins to the Masquerade celebrations at Ikpoba Hill. We thoroughly enjoyed the festivities and returned to the house absolutely worn out. By ten p.m. everyone had gone to bed due to exhaustion. Moreover, we knew that we had to get up early the next morning to organise the cleaning of the house, and to do our packing.

I fell asleep as soon as my head hit the pillow and started dreaming of the masquerade celebrations. In my dream, the masquerades came out flamboyantly dressed, dancing around the square and weaving through the crowd of people who had come to partake in the celebrations. The drummers dexterously beat their drums, and enthralled, my cousins and I danced in tune to the beat. The drummers spurred on by our enthusiastic dancing beat their drums faster and faster. I loved it and started dancing like someone possessed. By this time, I was in the middle of the square and people had formed a ring around me, cheering me on and chanting in tune to the beats. The masquerades joined me and we gyrated in unison. This continued for a while until one of the drummers started to beat his drum out of sync. Frowning, I stopped dancing to rebuke him, but he continued banging on his drum unperturbed. The other drummers stopped beating their drums as the banging from the errant drummer grew louder and louder until the square, and indeed the ground, reverberated with the force of his banging.

I jerked out of my bed startled. The banging was not coming from the drummer in my dream. It was real. I hastened out of bed and ran to the landing where I met Dad and Osagie. Mum was standing in the doorway of their room, her eyes wide with fear. Even before Dad told us what was going on, I guessed... armed robbers.

Confirming my suspicions, Dad whispered that there were armed men trying to break into the house. They were making a loud racket. Dad tried using the telephone to call the police but the telephone line had been cut. Iyen and Idehen had joined us on the landing by this time and he told all of us to go and hide as he did not know how long it would take for help to come.

Before we could spring into action, the house gave a shudder as the front door collapsed under the barrage and in poured a gang of men armed with guns, cutlasses, and machetes. They fanned out in different directions. I managed to count seven of them from my position at the top of the stairs before I beat a hasty retreat to my room, locked the door, and hid under my bed. Apparently everyone else had also locked their bedroom doors, because I heard simultaneous banging on the doors to all the bedrooms upstairs.

A voice called out and told us to open all doors immediately. "Osadolor, we know you are in there. We have your house surrounded, so there is no way for you to escape. You people should come out peacefully right now."

When there was no response, the voice continued, "If we have to break down these doors, I can assure you that you and your wife will bury all your children with your own hands."

Mum began to wail. I heard Dad murmuring something to her, but could not make out his precise words. A moment later, I heard the loud creak of my parent's bedroom door as it was opened. There was a short exchange between Dad and one of the robbers. My heart leapt when Dad told them only he and Mum were home.

"In that case, you would not mind us taking a look for ourselves. Anyone we find in this house apart from you and your wife shall be killed, and that should not bother you much since they will be trespassers who are here with neither your knowledge nor permission."

I heard Mum wail louder and Dad ask, "What do you want? You can have anything. Anything at all, just please leave my family alone. I have a lot of money. You can have it all. Come, let's go to my study. I'll show you where the money is."

"Sharrap," came the reply. "We will take what we like. Tell the people in the bedrooms to come out or else blood will flow here tonight." By this time, I had started praying.

"Please-", Dad began and I heard a thud. Mum screamed hysterically and I heard Dad groaning.

"Please, I beg you," Mum pleaded.

"Call them out. Right now," snarled the robber. "Call them out before I count to three," he continued. "Oneee... twoooo..."

"Osagie, Ameze, Iyen, Idehen. You children should come out now," Mum cried. "Please hurry up before they become angry."

I crawled out from underneath my bed and hastened to my bedroom door which I unlocked as quickly as my trembling fingers could allow. My legs felt like jelly and I was afraid that they would give way. I managed to make it out to the landing and saw my mother kneeling next to my father. He was sitting on the floor with blood pouring out of a gash on his temple.

"Daddy!" I screamed in alarm, rushing to his side.

"I am alright," he tried to reassure me with a shaky smile.

The robber who had been doing all the talking and who I assumed was their leader, ordered us downstairs. Mum helped Dad to his feet and as we proceeded downstairs, the lead robber ordered two others to carry out a thorough check of all the rooms upstairs.

Downstairs, we saw that the other robbers had been very busy. All Dad's electronic gadgets had been assembled in the front hall and the robbers were still hard at work amassing their loot as we were marched into the large front sitting room — which my parents used as a reception room. Mum continued to cry softly. Iyen was also weeping. I glared defiantly at the robbers. Three of them stood guarding us whilst others brought in the television sets from the bedrooms, Mum's jewellery and expensive wrappers, my father's suits, shoes, and wristwatches. The entertainment centre that Osagie received as a Christmas gift from Mum and Dad was not spared and neither was my PlayStation.

I felt an indescribable rage seize me, but there was nothing I could do. In this state, the true meaning of the phrase 'impotent rage' finally dawned on me, as that was what my rage was, impotent. I seethed inwardly, hatred burning in my heart. I glanced at Osagie and saw the same emotions mirrored in his eyes. My throat felt constricted like a boulder was lodged within it and I felt tears start to well up at the back of my eyes, but mentally tried to shoo them away. I was not going to give any of the thieving bastards the satisfaction of seeing me cry.

The lead robber walked around Dad and said, "So Mr. Big Man, who is the big shot now? You think you are better than everybody ehn? You come to Benin-City with your useless family and think that everything must come to a halt because you are in town? You give money to people like we are all beggars waiting to scramble for some little crumbs that would fall from your table. How big do you feel now in front of your family?"

"There is no need for any of this," Dad said in a subdued voice.

He looked deflated as the robber continued in a derisory tone, "Mr. Big Man, say something, or are you going to continue sitting there staring like a zombie?"

He paced from one end of the room to the other. "It is people like you who are destroying this country. Only you and your family are enjoying all this wealth. You are very greedy. Did you hear what I said Osadolor? I said you are very greedy. There are millions of people suffering in this country. Millions are crying everyday from poverty and dying of hunger, but people like you don't care about that. You go about in your fancy clothes and flashy cars thinking you are superior to the rest of us," the robber ranted.

"I give to the poor all the time," Dad said.

"Sharrap," barked the robber. "Who gave you permission to talk, ehn? You give handouts to people. Mere crumbs.

How much do you pay the labourers who work on your cocoa plantation? They slave for you day in day out under the hot sun, but you rake in the cash. You just use them anyhow you like and do not care that they are human beings like you. My father worked for you for seventeen years," he continued. "Seventeen whole years of his life. What did he have to show for it? Absolutely nothing. He died in penury. A pauper, with nothing to show for all the years of hard labour. You callously made him redundant when his arthritic fingers could not work fast enough. Yet you go around like a mini-god. Look at my friend over there." He pointed at one of the robbers standing by the door. "His mother who was a picker at your plantation was sacked just because she helped herself to a few measly cocoa pods to augment the beggarly wages you were paying her. Nobody cared that she was the only breadwinner of her family and had seven children to feed. Nobody cared that she had slaved for you for more than twelve years. She was not given any warning. No query, no suspension, no fair-hearing; only dismissal, plain and simple."

He paused, and then asked quietly, as if talking to a friend, "What have you ever done for your community?" Dad said nothing. "Am I not talking to you Osadolor?"

"I know what I do for my community and I know how many people I have helped," Dad retorted angrily. "I do not have to go round broadcasting it to everyone nor do I need to beat my chest about it. You people have gotten what you came here for, so please just take your loot and leave me and my family in peace."

"Loot? Loot?" the robber asked in an angry yet incredulous tone. "Are you calling us robbers?"

I took a long look at the ranting robber. He had a crazed look in his eyes like he was high.

"Capone, make we show am how robbers dey deal with people like him and him family?" another robber addressed the lead robber in Pidgin English. "Me, I like this him pikin well, well. She fine no be small," he continued, advancing towards me. I could not believe my ears and glared furiously at him. "Fine girl, how are you?" he asked, cupping his hand beneath my chin.

"Get your stinking hand off me," I screamed, slapping his hand away.

"Leave her alone," Dad roared. "Leave my daughter alone right now!"

Capone threw his head back and laughed maniacally. "Or what? What will you do Osadolor? What can you do? I can wipe out your entire family in the space of two minutes."

Mum, who had ceased crying, began wailing again. She started pleading with the robbers. "Please do not hurt us. Have mercy on us, I beg you. You can take everything, just leave us alone. You can take the cars, even the house. We won't call the police, I swear."

Capone laughed again. "Nobody wants to hurt anyone," he said. "My friend here likes your daughter, that's all. Don't you think he is good looking enough for her?" When no one replied, he asked, "So you think that she is too good for him or that she is better than him?" Still there was no response. "Answer me!" he snapped at Mum.

"I did not say that O," Mum wailed. "Please do not hurt us."

"Sharrap."

"Do not shout at my mother," Osagie bellowed back at him. Immediately, one of the other robbers lunged at him and whacked him across the face with the butt of his rifle. I heard a crunch as Osagie's nose broke and blood streamed down his face. "You have killed my son O," Mum screamed hysterically.

"I said Sharrap," Capone shouted.

Dad addressed Capone. "If you people lay another finger on any of my family, I swear to God, you will live to regret it."

"Is that so?" Capone beckoned to the other robber who liked me and said, "Corporal, take the girl. She is yours. Do whatever you want with her." While saying this, he pulled out a little pistol from the waistband of his trousers and slung his rifle by its strap over his shoulder. Turning back to Dad and levelling his pistol at him, he said "Now let's see what you can do."

Corporal looked like he could not believe his luck. "Capone, thank you," he said as he approached me, smirking and licking his lips. Leering lasciviously, he lunged for me and grabbed my nightie at the neck in his grubby paws, yanking it downwards. The nightie tore like it was made from paper and my breasts came spilling out, on show for all and sundry to see. When this happened, the other robbers cheered while I screamed. I started kicking and punching him as hard as I could, whilst using one hand to try to cover up my shame.

This is not happening to me. It is just a bad dream and I will soon wake up, I kept telling myself. He grabbed my knickers and ripped them off.

"Daddy! Daddy! Please help me," I screamed, sobbing and still trying to fight him off. The brute picked me up and hurled me against the wall. My head ricocheted off the wall and for a brief moment, all I saw was a blank void. I was also winded and could barely put up a fight, so I crossed my legs as tightly as I could. Corporal tried to pry them apart without much success, as I crossed them tighter whilst squirming from side to side.

He smacked me very hard across my face a few times. One of my teeth became loose. I could taste something strange and metallic in my mouth and there was a roaring noise in my ears. I was in agony, but still managed to keep my legs clamped shut.

"Punch her in the thigh, you moron," I heard a voice say from somewhere that seemed very far away, and surely enough, I felt pain explode in my thighs as the brute landed heavy blows on them. My thigh muscles went slack and refused to obey the commands that my brain was desperately and frantically passing through to them.

"Open Sesame," Corporal guffawed with satisfaction as he used one hand and his knees to part my thighs, while he used his other hand to undo his zipper.

Corporal never got to complete this act because I saw Dad move swiftly. The heavy vase that had lain on the coffee table came crashing down on his head. He slumped on top of me, blood from a cut on his head dripping onto my bosom. I heard the loud deafening boom of a gun going off. Dad came crashing down less than a foot away from me.

Screams rang in my ears. Mine was one of them. Dad lay still, face down near me.

"Sharrap," Capone shouted, but nobody paid him heed.

"I said Sharrap!"

Mum, still screaming, was now beside Dad; tears streaming down her face. I was screaming too as I tried to dislodge the mammoth weight that was threatening to crush me. I continued to scream through the robber's words and my screams drowned out whatever he was saying.

Capone fired his gun twice in quick succession into the ceiling. Showers of plaster rained down on us and we became silent.

"I will not say this again. If anyone starts to make a noise here, that person shall not live to see daylight. Do you understand?" Petrified, nobody moved nor said a word. "I said do you understand?" he thundered.

"Yes," we all chorused.

"Good."

Gesturing to his comrades, he said, "Take Corporal to the van." Two of the other robbers, lifted the brute off me and carried him outside. I tried to cover up my nakedness as best as I could with my tattered nightie. I saw that the fracas had brought more of the robbers into the house and they all crowded the doorway leading into the sitting-room.

I crawled to my father and breathed a sigh of relief when I saw that his eyes were open and blinking. Mum was sobbing as quietly as she could. Osagie looked ashen and grim. The twins clutched one another tightly, crying silently. I gave silent thanks to God that Dad was still alive and that the brute had not succeeded in raping me.

My thanksgiving was however untimely, as Capone marched over to Dad and pulled him up by the collar of his pyjamas. Dad tottered on his legs and I noticed that the first shot I had heard had hit him in his right leg. He swayed and came crashing back down to the floor. Capone viciously grabbed him again by the collar and put his gun to Dad's temple.

"Get up now you stupid bastard," he yelled, "or I swear on my mother's life that I will blow your brains all over your family."

Dad stood balancing on his one good leg.

"So, you think you are a hero ehn? Do you think you are a match for me or any of my men? You are lucky that Corporal is not dead because I would have wiped out your entire family before your very eyes," he thundered. "You don't want another man to fuck your daughter," he continued crudely. "You want to fuck her yourself ehn? That is exactly what you shall do here tonight since you don't want anyone else to do so."

Time stood still.

I stopped believing that God existed and stared incredulously at Capone. He had a crazed glint in his eyes and the slant of his mouth turned down in a sneer. The angles of his jaw were set determinedly. To me he looked like the Devil.

I felt like I was caught up in the most awful nightmare. I cursed my father's decision to build a house in a location where the nearest neighbour was almost a mile away.

On hearing his words, Mum shrieked and jumped to her feet crying. She ran over to Capone, got on her knees in supplication and clutched at the legs of his trousers. "Please, don't do this to my family. Please don't ruin my family. Kill me instead."

"Shut up Ivie!" Dad snapped at her. "Why are you pleading with the lunatic? Do you think I am going to sleep with my own daughter?" Turning to Capone, he said, "That is not going to happen. You will have to kill me. I am a grown man and I am not afraid to die." Turning to each of us, he told us that he loved us and told Osagie to take care of us as he was going to be the man of the house, then he raised his hands in a gesture of surrender and closed his eyes waiting for the hail of bullets. I shut my eyes dreading the sound of another gunshot.

"Capone, make we waste am?" One of the other robbers asked.

"No, no, no," Capone said. "Do not kill him." I breathed a sigh of relief and opened my eyes to see him move within inches of Dad.

Very calmly, he spoke to Dad in a quiet voice, "Osadolor, you have to get it into your thick skull that you will do as I say whether you want to or not."

"I am not sleeping with my own daughter no matter what you do to me. You can go to hell." Dad spat at him.

"Is that so? We shall see." Turning to his men but addressing no one in particular, he barked, "Bring the girl here." Two men detached themselves from the group and walked towards me as I scrambled behind Mum screaming no.

Osagie sprang to his feet in my defence shouting, "Leave my sister alone you stinking pervert."

A loud boom sounded and Osagie went down clutching his arm and shouting with pain.

"That is your second warning tonight, you fool," yelled Capone. "You won't live to tell the story of your folly if you should try this a third time."

Mum, still on her knees with my arms clutched tightly around her waist once again, started to plead with Capone. He ignored her and shouted at his two men who were standing near Mum and me.

"Did I not tell you to bring the girl here?"

The two robbers grabbed me, with one prying my arms away from where they were locked around Mum's waist. I was dragged to where Capone stood before Dad and dumped at his feet.

"Do as I say right now," Capone ordered Dad.

"No."

"I repeat, do as I say Osadolor."

"You can say it as many times as you like, you maniac. I am not going to sleep with my own daughter."

"Do not say I did not warn you…" Turning to his men, he ordered, "Bring the little boy to me."

The two goons who had dumped me at his feet, rushed over to the corner of the room where Iyen and Idehen were huddled together and grabbed Idehen by the arms, dragging him towards their leader. Frightened, Iyen clung to Idehen sobbing desperately and one of the goons landed her with a backhand slap which sent her sprawling back into the corner.

Enraged, Osagie charged at the robber. The charge took the robber entirely by surprise and the force of Osagie's body propelled him backwards and sent him crashing into the wall where he sank to the floor.

For the fifth time that night, a gun went off.

I shut my eyes, then I opened them, hoping, praying that everything had been a figment of my imagination. The scene remained the same. It was no imagination and neither was it a nightmare. Osagie lay slumped half on top of the robber he had charged into. There was blood and flesh all over the robber and the wall behind him. There was a huge gaping wound in what remained of Osagie's neck where the bullet had blown almost half of his neck away. The robber pushed Osagie off him, and from my position I could see that his eyes were wide open. There was a look of surprise or shock in them, like he had not expected to be shot from behind. His mouth was agape.

Dad lunged at Capone and he was shot in the arm.

"Bring the little boy to me," the robber snarled, repeating his earlier order.

Attempting to cry softly, Idehen got to his feet and shuffled to Capone who turned to one of the other robbers clustered at the door and barked, "Major, go to the van and get me the industrial hammer." The robber who was addressed as Major ran off and returned with a sledge hammer.

Nodding towards Idehen, Capone told Major to smash his big toe with the hammer. Major seemed hesitant to carry out the order and the leader said, "Remember your sister Onome and how she died because your father could not afford to take her to the hospital after this bastard Osadolor had sacked him. Remember also your brother Osarugwe who is a multiple amputee because he was forced to hawk wares on the express road when your father lost his job, and remember your father, who took his own life because he felt shame when he could no longer provide for his family."

Major forcefully brought the hammer down, not once, but twice on Idehen's left foot, shattering the big toe. Idehen let out a blood curdling scream and crumpled to the floor clutching the foot that housed his now mangled toe.

Idehen's anguished cry must have reached Mum somewhere in the subconscious as she came awake with a startled cry of her own. She started sobbing and babbling incoherently.

Unmoved, Capone addressed Dad again, "For each time you refuse to do as I order, one of your family members will lose a body part. My patience is infinite as I have waited for this day for a very long time. Your arrogance will be your undoing Osadolor, and in the end it may cost you your entire family."

Dad remained on the floor, sitting with his head bowed to his chest. He was silent, unmoving, as if he had not heard what was said.

"You are a fool," Capone said. Then dipping his hand into his pocket, he walked over to where Mum was. He pulled out a Stanley knife from his pocket. Startled at the sight of the knife and dreading what he might do with it, I crawled towards him and spoke up whilst grabbing the leg of his trousers as Mum had done previously in supplication.

"Please don't hurt my mother," I begged. "You can bring back your Corporal friend. I will sleep with him if you want. Please."

"Don't beg me, beg your father. He has the power to make everything stop," he said turning to Dad. "Osadolor, won't you listen to your daughter's pleas?"

Dad sat immobile; silent.

Tucking his pistol into the waistband of his trousers, Capone kicked me off his leg and pounced on Mum. In the blink of an eye, the front of Mum's nightie had been cut away. Mum sat rooted to her spot. She was unflinching and stared at Capone with tears streaming down her face. Her lips moved, but it was not to plead for mercy as she had previously done. When she spoke, a string of curses, which revealed her tortured mental state, emanated from her mouth.

"You will never know happiness in your life. As you have torn my family apart, so shall your family be scattered before your very eyes. The hand that robbed me of my first born child shall turn upon itself in betrayal. You will know no peace. The eyes that stood by and watched this evil being perpetrated against me and my family shall be extinguished in their youth. You all shall grope in darkness as you wander the earth destitute..."

As she carried on with her curses, Capone whacked her across the face, prompting one of the other robbers to speak up. "Ehi," he called, addressing Capone. Capone did not answer him. "Ehi, that's enough. I think we should leave now. We have gotten what we came for. Let's go."

Capone turned around angrily whipping out his pistol. "Who the hell are you to tell me what to do or when to stop?" he yelled waving the pistol around dangerously. "We stop only when I say so, not a moment before, and I say we do not leave here until Osadolor does as he is told. Is that understood?" A few of the other robbers nodded. They looked either petrified or intimidated.

"Osadolor, this is your last chance before I descend on your wife."

There was no response from Dad.

Capone turned back to Mum and sliced off her left nipple. Mum screamed, holding her blood covered breast and started heaping more curses on him. I prayed to wake up from the nightmare, but I was to have no reprieve.

Capone tossed Mum's severed nipple into Dad's lap and said that he would be moving on to Iyen next.

I knew I had to act fast, so I crawled to Dad and begged him to do as Capone had ordered. He did not move and I started to shake and hit at him. Looking into his face, I saw that my father was no longer there. The man staring back at me with tears running unchecked down his face was a stranger.

Finally, Dad moved slightly. My voice had eventually succeeded in penetrating his brain. Sobbing, he started to apologise to me, to my Mum, to Idehen, to Iyen and especially to Osagie who lay stone dead a few feet away. He apologised for being a failure as a father, for failing to protect us when we needed his protection the most. He wept and wept and begged Capone to take his life, but his pleas were ignored. The inevitability of the situation stared him starkly in the face and he resigned himself to the abomination which he must now commit.

He was a broken man.

The robbers led by Capone, left the house almost quietly. There was a solemnity in their departure.

Coming out of my ruminations, I take a last look at the red flags flapping in the night breeze. It is a beautiful night with the moon shining brightly and illuminating the beach.

I look around the beach as far as my eyes can see and am happy to observe that I am alone. The slight breeze which had been blowing inland off the Atlantic has picked up a bit and I shiver a little, rubbing my hands up my arms and feeling goose-bumps on them.

Determinedly, I walk into the sea before my courage deserts me. It is still quite warm from the hot day that ended a few hours ago and I can feel the water enveloping me, comforting me, encouraging me to lay down my burden and advance deeper and deeper inside. I am not afraid, I am not scared. I know that I will be joining my big brother soon. For the first time in almost a fortnight, I feel at peace. I am calm and totally in control of my destiny.

I advance into the sea until my feet stop touching the sand below. The waves are rising higher and higher and a few times, they cover my head. I try to remember not to float instinctively and I let the powerful waves drag me further and further out to sea. I close my eyes and surrender myself to the command of the sea, knowing that all my troubles will soon be over. As I am being dragged under, my mind involuntarily and of its own accord says a prayer to a God I had stopped believing in.

Father into your hands I commit my Spirit, Amen.

Born in Lagos, Nigeria and descendant of kin from the West Indies, Sierra Leone and the Republic of Benin, Ayodele Morocco-Clarke is a Nigerian of mixed heritage currently living in the UK. Her prose and poetry have appeared in numerous print and online journals and anthologies including the 2011 Caine Prize anthology. Her short story 'When the Chips are Down' was short-listed for the International Students' Short Story Competition in 2010.

Water Wahala

Isaac Neequaye

Kweku Kyere whistled strains from Yaa Amponsah, as he shut the door and sauntered into the living room. Agyapomaa was slouched in front of the TV engrossed in a sitcom. Still dressed in her work clothes, it was evident she hadn't been home long. "Hello Sweetie, how did your day go?" he called across cheerily.

Shifting her attention from the TV she smiled sweetly. "It went well. And you, how was it at Don's Place?" Agyapomaa was always curious about how he spent those few after work hours on Friday evenings before getting home.

A grin peeked out and slowly spread across his face as Kweku placed his briefcase on the dining table. "Not bad. Not bad at all."

Don's Place was a popular hangout for Accra yuppies, where he liked to unwind after a gruelling week. The heat, traffic, and demands of his job as construction manager for an Italian construction company, combined to drain him completely. It provided the perfect setting to relax and catch up on happenings around town at the beginning of the weekend.

Agyapomaa's face lit up as he handed her a take-away pack of grilled pork. He couldn't help chuckling.

It wasn't clear what kind of sound, if any, crossed his ears as he settled down to his favourite homecoming routine, but he kept going. Deftly manoeuvring his feet he pried off his shoes and jerked at his socks. Freeing his feet from their day long confinement was a routine he enjoyed tremendously. Again that sound as he tucked the shoes away. He glanced up, wondering whether it came from her nose or throat.

"Kweku, we're out of water oh... We need to buy some."

"Humph!" He sat up straight, instantly alert. "Are you sure?" he questioned warily in a tone hovering someplace between a whisper and a hiss.

Agyapomaa's mouth was full, but the disdain in her eyes as she munched away said it all.

Usually Kweku kept a close eye on their water situation, but with both their kids away at boarding school he'd ceded the monitoring to his wife. "How much do we have left?"

"Uhm, enough for a bath or two."

He winced. "Eish! Is that all?"

A heavy silence, punctuated only by the sound of Agyapomaa's munching hung between them for a moment. "Ok," he said, and sighed. "I'll arrange something tomorrow."

"If I cook we won't be able to bath, and if we bath I won't be able to cook," Agyapomaa said gazing steadily at him. Her point made, she turned her attention back to the TV.

The three large beers Kweku gulped down earlier that evening had lifted his spirits immensely. But the cheeriness with which he'd arrived home ebbed away like water seeping into parched earth without a trace. In its wake a wretched, slow-burning irritation began smouldering. Running out of water always had that effect on him.

Monitoring the family's water usage seemed a fairly straightforward chore, and so how did she always manage to bungle it, Kweku fumed, his breath spurting out in short furious bursts. At times like these he couldn't resist the resentful feelings that welled up in his chest against his wife, and to a lesser extent their daughter — the two people who used the most water in the house. It didn't matter that Mansa was away at school. The irksome thing too was that whenever they ran out of water Agyapomaa only announced it and sat back, waiting for him to work some magic. The kids being at school meant that his son, Yaw, wasn't available to run this errand. Kweku would have to do it himself. The irony gnawed at him; Yaw who used very little water — he welcomed every opportunity to skip a bath — being called upon again to go search for water that his mother and sister lapped up like a pair of mermaids.

He opened his mouth to tick Agyapomaa off for not alerting him earlier to the dwindling store of water, but ended up shutting it like a guppy, without uttering a word. I should have known better, he groused silently. She was always like that. Whenever the matter was left in her hands she always waited until they'd practically run out of water before speaking up. Now she'd pitched them all into a bind. Agyapomaa normally cooked over the weekend, and he'd learned over the years not to disrupt her schedule unless it was absolutely necessary.

Even though he attended an evangelical Christian church and professed creationism, Kweku Kyere had gradually come to believe in Darwinism. The development of a mental water meter to track his family's water usage was a vital step in his evolutionary journey. Everyone in Adentan Housing Bottom, their neighbourhood, went through this phase that imbued them with sharpened water management skills. Well, almost everyone. Agyapomaa had just proven again that the only way to effectively monitor the family's water usage was for Kweku to do it himself, even though he spent so much time away from home. As fallible as such mental man-made instruments are, occasionally his water meter let him down. Angrily he chased away any such recollections.

No Adentan resident could honestly claim to be unaffected by the unavailability of water. It was simply ubiquitous, never far from one's mind, an issue that stressed everybody out in different ways. Kweku considered it particularly undignified to have to think through a choice of using the toilet or dashing out into the garden to pee.

Years earlier, when they first moved to Adentan, the taps flowed once a week. In time the frequency reduced to once a fortnight, then once a month, and then once about every six weeks, before dwindling even further apart. It would have been nice after all these years to be able to say that water flowed through the taps once in a blue moon, but the reality was that the moon at Adentan was a pale yellow colour. The last time water flowed through the taps must have been nine months ago.

All the efforts the Housing Bottom Residents' Association undertook to pressure the authorities into addressing the problem amounted to nought. The nebulous entity called the Ghanaman Water Company was either deaf, blind, mute, or perhaps all three, it never even acknowledged a single one of their many complaints and suggestions.

The advent of party politics hadn't helped either. All the candidates that vied for the new Adentan seat — when it was hived off from the huge Ashaiman constituency — strived to outdo each other in pronouncing spirited promises to chase up the water company to fix the problem once and for all. Since winning, the MP — a short, balding, former businessman — had discovered that commissioning schools and chairing church functions yielded more opportunities for favourable press coverage. He had even taken to staring straight ahead whenever he passed by in his chauffeured vehicle, like someone with a stiff neck. Ultimately Kweku couldn't help wondering how much influence the MP actually wielded, or indeed, could command. Nevertheless their MP had made very audacious assurances on a public platform, and the Housing Bottom community needed someone to blame and bash for letting them down.

He made a mental note while getting ready for bed not to flush the toilet during the night, no matter how rancid the stench in the bathroom got. The weather was warm and for a long while he tossed and turned trying to fall asleep. It wasn't until he realised how his mood was driving his inability to fall asleep that he tried to look on the bright side. At least his daughter Mansa was away and he wouldn't have to battle over her insistence on bathing no matter what.

Though he set the alarm for five a.m. Kweku cursed it for rousing him. He felt a bit groggy, as if the previous night's beers were now taking effect. Wearily he dragged his body out of bed and began searching for his clothes. The income from the private construction projects he undertook during the weekend was vital to balancing his family's budget, and it wasn't until he was done with them that he could see to other weekend chores.

"Don't forget the water," Agyapomaa rasped, as he slipped on his shoes in the pre-dawn darkness.

A bolt of anger jolted Kweku fully awake. "Okay," he muttered, and then in a slightly lower tone, "If only you took your own advice." There was no way he could forget even if he wanted to. Not after holding his nose as he took an early morning pee. The toilet smelled like a boarding school urinal; you only needed to follow the stench to find your way there.

Outside, Kweku trudged through a sharp early morning breeze to his car. The Kyeres were one of the first families to settle at Adentan Housing Bottom when the estate was released to buyers twelve years previously. Only a handful of houses were completed at the time and Kweku supervised the finishing touches to their home himself. In those days the chilly early morning breeze draught sweeping down from the Akwapim hills was invigorating. He was bursting with the confidence and optimism that normally accompanies the purchase of a first home. The timing couldn't have been better; just ten years out of university, recently married with two young kids, newly promoted to senior quantity surveyor. They were the envy of all their friends. Now, given the myriad estate developments that had since sprung up, it was doubtful whether anyone would trade places with them.

At that time, in spite of having had two kids in quick succession, Agyapomaa could still have won a beauty pageant or two. She carved a deep impression in Kweku's heart when he first met her; for weeks on end he ran every errand for his office that had to do with hers, just so that he could catch glimpses of her. Then she was the director's secretary at the Department of Urban Roads. Eventually gathering his wits he made a determined play for her affections and chewed his nails while she coyly hedged about for a couple of weeks before consenting.

His friends almost succeeded in throwing a spanner into the spokes though, teasing that he'd only be harvesting where the rich contractors — of whom Agyapomaa knew so many — had sowed. They all had to get past her to see the boss and who knew whether she was fooling around with one or even several of them? Those fears were quickly dispelled when they began dating. Agyapomaa proved a most able gatekeeper over her charms. It was soon unambiguously manifest that he would never get past her defences without putting a ring on her finger. "You can go to hell," she spat at him when he tried the 'certificate of fertility' shenanigan; she would never, ever, consider becoming pregnant before being wedded. It took him four weeks to muster the courage to come begging, and the most humiliating part was having to face her mother. If only he could have turned back the clock and wiped the slate clean.

They hadn't been married long before Kweku began to understand why his wife was such a highly rated secretary. You couldn't forget anything if it was her business to remind you. The converse, particularly when it came to water, was different.

Kweku dug into his briefcase and fished out his old dog-eared diary. Before settling down to thumb through it for Danso's — his water deliverer's — number, he took his time to polish off the Hausa koko porridge and akara, that he'd bought on his way home, savouring every bite.

The kind of people that pursued Danso's profession weren't noted for courteousness. Because so many people depended upon them for water — particularly the wealthier residents of inner Eastlands who had no fixed occupations or discernible sources of income — they had grown pointedly arrogant. But the circumstances of habitation at Adentan conspired to cement the residents' dependence on water tankers. They had no choice but to bear it. So Kweku was astounded to hear the word "please" at the other end of the line. It didn't take long though, for their conversation to revert to norm.

"Danso, ahbeg, I need some water. Urgently."

"Oh! Only that?"

"Yes," obviously, as except for water he had no business with Danso.

"At your house eh?"

"Yes."

"At Adentan Housing Bottom eh?"

"The same place. I'm still there." Kweku strived to keep the edge out of his voice.

"Ok Massa Kweku. You see, I promise, but not right away. Someone at Eastlands has already chartered me and I am filling for him. So let's say in about two hours. If it delays at all, add thirty to forty-five minutes."

"That's perfect with me. Erm, I hope the price hasn't changed?"

"As for the price, deɛ, it is the same... maybe something small for the boys."

"No problem. I'll be waiting for you. But Danso..."

"Yes Massa."

"It's urgent oh... Madam is sitting on my neck."

"Don't worry Massa. This one, na small problem. I go be there, I promise, say, by ten-thirty, eleven, eleven-thirty. I go be there sharp."

Kweku exhaled as he hung up, thankful that he'd been able to sort it out so quickly. As far as he and his fellow Adentan residents were concerned the mobile phone ranked ahead by miles as the greatest invention of the twentieth century. The mobile phone-free days of past were a nightmare, particularly if you also didn't have a car. The Kyeres' couldn't imagine how they had gotten by in the past. The truth Kweku knew but would never vocalise was that it was too painful to remember. If only they could find a way to be independent of the foul-mouthed roughnecks, who called themselves the Sands Down Tanker Drivers' Union, they would consider themselves truly blessed.

After toying briefly with the idea of taking a shower he decided against it. Hell hath no fury like Agyapomaa's cooking interrupted. It was 9.15 a.m. when he checked his watch.

"You've been able to organise some water?" Agyapomaa asked hopefully as he helped her carry the shopping into the kitchen.

Inwardly Kweku groaned. His wife had a sweet way of applying pressure. "Danso is bringing us some. Said we should expect him by eleven thereabouts."

"Wonderful. By then I should be finishing up the cooking. Then we can both take a nice, long shower." She winked at him.

He couldn't help the broad grin that split his face.

Hard as he tried Kweku found it impossible to concentrate on anything at home. Kitchen noises wove in and out of his ears, grating his nerves, until their waning tempo suggested that Agyapomaa was at the tidying up stage. And still the water hadn't shown up.

"Agyapomaa, I'll be back in about thirty minutes, okay? I'm checking my mail at Junior's." With that Kweku pulled on a pair of sandals and slipped outside.

He flipped out his cell phone immediately after he shut the gate. "Oh Massa Kweku, it's not me oh," Danso shrieked after the fifth ring. "The loading guys are just delaying us here. I got back long ago but haven't been able to load. I am next in the line now. So let's say in an hour's time I should be at your place."

"One hour?"

"Massa Kweku, the water will come ri...ght now. Everything is under control."

"Ok Danso, I'm waiting." He cut the call, noting the time on his cell phone. 11.40 a.m. Junior's Internet Cafe was the best place to kill some time. Staying out of Agyapomaa's way was the prudent thing to do, at least until the tanker showed up with its precious cargo.

Agyapomaa was directing their house-help Ewurama to mop the kitchen with the last bucketful of water in the house, when she heard someone shoving at the front gate. Quickly she darted to a window, her hopes rising in anticipation. Thrusting aside the curtain she peeked through, only to spy Kweku shuffling in and peering sheepishly around the yard as if searching for a hidden water tanker.

Her husband's indignation at the fact that the water had practically run out before she raised the alarm had been palpable throughout their home since Friday night. Truly, she had it in mind to alert him last Sunday that they were running low, but a long phone call from her sister in Canada diverted her attention, and somehow it slipped. It was a genuine slip, like every human being made every now and again. Nevertheless Kwekus's brooding silent anger, like a slowly ticking bomb, poisoned the atmosphere at home. Sometimes he just about drove the rest of the family up the wall – like the time he threatened to go on trek, leaving them all behind without any water. That tyrannical streak... it was the last thing she would have imagined when he was courting her. Curiously too it seemed to manifest only when they argued about water. But he'd had all morning, more than enough time in her opinion, to do something, and now beneath her apparent calm composure her insides had also begun bristling. How much effort did it take to summon up a water tanker anyway?

Every weekday, from the moment her eyes cracked open at dawn, she and Kweku slid into well-choreographed roles, honed over more than a decade, in the mad rush to make it out of home and beat the Adentan traffic to work. Every other consideration, everything, including the level of water in their tank, was discarded in that all-consuming pursuit. And almost invariably, neither of them remembered as they trudged back home, exhausted from the day's exertions and further ground down by the numbing traffic jams. Even on days that she remembered, she was invariably too weary to go poking about the backyard at night. No wonder Kweku was always so eager to hand over that responsibility to her as soon as the kids went off to school. If it were so simple why didn't he continue doing it himself? Sometimes, deep in sleep, he even mumbled about water.

"Hasn't the water tanker shown up yet?" Kweku asked, poking his head around the kitchen door.

She grimaced, before opening her mouth. "You would have seen signs, not so? Are you sure he's coming?"

"He said he'd be here by noon."

"Look Kweku, you'd better go out and get someone else to supply us water. These tanker guys aren't reliable. Rogues they are... all of them."

"But Danso is reliable."

In spite of her resolve Agyapomaa felt her cool slipping. "Are you sure his tanker is even on the road? Have you seen it?"

"No, but Agyapomaa, you know Danso. Why do you doubt him now?"

"Me! I've never trusted him. That's how they all are. He can't keep us waiting at his convenience. What manner of kwasiasem is that?"

Kweku drew in a sharp breath; apparently he was taken aback at the vehemence in her voice and the reference to foolishness.

"The water he's supplying isn't free, is it?" she asked.

Kweku shook his head from side to side.

"Then it doesn't matter if we find someone else to supply us, does it? How am I supposed to bath? How am I supposed to clean the house? What if we got visitors just now? I've now piled on the smell of food to more than a day's sweat, and you think I should bear it nicely because you want to maintain your friendship with a tanker driver?"

Kweku inhaled deeply, and seemed to think for a moment.

Agyapomaa wouldn't let up. "What at all do you want to happen before you go out and get us some water? Just how much money are you trying to save that I should go about my own house like a street sweeper?"

Without a word he turned and slunk away.

When Kweku returned, mumbling into his cell phone, Agyapomaa was waiting, her arms folded across her chest, "Danso's just finished loading and will be setting off shortly," he announced.

"So he hasn't even left yet? Hey!" She clapped her hands in a quick short burst. "Kweku look for another tanker to bring us water. Don't waste any more time with this your Danso."

"Agyaps, please. He's on his way. I'll see what to do if he doesn't arrive within the hour."

"Another hour? Kweku, I know a fraud when I hear one. Forget about him and find someone else." She spun on her heels and stalked off.

"Agyaps, how can you say that?" he called after her retreating rear. Normally a stimulant for naughty thoughts, Agyapomaa's rear wiggled a firm, angry rebuke. Divergent urges of exasperation and rage battled for dominance within Kweku's chest. Agyapomaa's temper was bearable so long as you weren't at the receiving end. But this, the sight of her working up an angry lather, shot darts of rage coursing through his body! Despite the fact that she was to blame for the whole mess she was attacking him like it was

215

his fault entirely. And in spite of the situation the aroma wafting from the kitchen was making his tummy grumble.

"Do you need me to do anything for you? I'm heading towards Tetteh Quarshie?" Kweku didn't expect a response to the proffered olive branch. When incensed, Agyapomaa was equally good at the silent treatment.

"Yes, please," Agyapomaa answered, in a tone all sweet and sugary. "Could you please pick up some money from Auntie Francina for me? I gave her some shoes to sell and she says the money's ready. I don't want it to stay with her too long."

Kweku didn't need to speak. Unwillingness was plastered all over his face.

"Please. It's just along the way. I'd planned to do it myself this afternoon, but I can't go there like this, can I?" With her hands Agyapomaa tried to waft food fumes from her body in his direction. "It's my money; otherwise I wouldn't have bothered."

"Is she expecting you?"

"No, but I'll call to let her know you're coming." She dashed off in search of her cell phone.

But for the fact that it involved money, he would have found a way to turn her down. The road to Frafraha, where Francina lived, was so atrocious he wept for his car anytime he used it.

But something else was eating at him as Kweku grabbed his car keys. Danso's last words. "I'll be on my way ri...ght now." That was the second time he'd said that. Why did it make him feel uneasy?

Francina was waiting when he arrived and straight-away handed him a bulky brown envelope.

"That's three million cedis," she said.

He tore it open to find six bundles of shrink-wrapped five thousand cedi notes stared back at him. "Thank you," he said, nodding.

"Won't you get down?" she asked, surprised. "Let me offer you a drink, please."

"No thanks, Francina. We're out of water and I'll be a dead man if I don't find a tanker before the day is over. I have to run off right away."

He winked and gunned the engine, wondering as her house faded into the distance whether Fancina would have smelled that he hadn't washed all day.

It was hot and sweltering, and his shirt clung uncomfortably to his skin as Kweku navigated his way to the tanker loading bay. He was also becoming increasingly conscious of the odour from his unwashed body. The water tankers that served their area usually loaded their supplies at a water company office just off the Tetteh Quarshie roundabout, a huge interchange that constituted a very popular landmark.

Taking advantage of the slow moving traffic Kweku dialled home as he waited his turn at the Adentan police checkpoint. "Has the tanker arrived?" he demanded when Ewurama answered.

"No. No one has come."

"Okay, thanks."

Next, he dialled Danso's number. His phone was off. Kweku stared at his phone in horror, his jaw dropping, and almost ran into the car in front of him. Twice more he redialled and got the same message: "the mobile number you are trying to reach is either off or out of service range." The stirrings of unease he'd felt earlier condensed into a tightly coiled spring of apprehension.

The tanker loading bay was a makeshift clearing next to the water company offices. It appeared unusually tranquil when he arrived, as if the drivers had taken off on lunch break. Perhaps they were napping, he thought. But something didn't feel right — no one hailed him or ran up to his car. Usually the boys — touts canvassing for business for the various tankers — swarmed around prospective customers like vultures drawn to a kill.

The foreboding that all wasn't well intensified as he strode briskly to the nearest tanker. Both its doors were wide open and strains of 'Me dofo a daadae me' spilled out. High up in the cab the driver was hunched over the wheel squinting into the rear view mirror; with a razor in his right hand he was carefully sculpting his beard. So engrossed was he that Kweku crept up on him unnoticed.

"Hello. I'm looking for Danso, one of your colleagues."

The man scowled when he peered down. He took his time, sizing Kweku up as if deciding whether or not to give him the time of day. "Danso?" he grunted after a moment. "And why are you now coming? He should have closed by now."

Closed? Kweku felt a knot of apprehension explode in his gut. Could Danso be on his way to Adentan? It must have shown on his face because the driver's tone was filled with concern when he spoke again, "Why, is there a problem?"

"He is bringing me water but is still yet to show up. That's why I'm here."

"Danso has loaded several times today but as for now, I can't tell where he is. Let me see." Pivoting his huge torso around he bellowed across the clearing at his colleagues, "Hey, anyone seen Danso?" A yawning silence reflected back at them. It wasn't clear what those waving at them meant. "Massa, this one na trouble for you oh! We have closed for the day. Danso's friends, erm... I mean those close to him, have also closed and gone already."

Kweku was stunned. Suddenly conscious of sweat trickling down his back, along his spine, he also felt an uncomfortable moistness in his armpits. "You've... closed?"

"Yes, we don' close. Saturday we close for two o'clock. You see how this place make quiet? Everybody don' go already. I just finished loading and am resting before I deliver my last load."

"Please," Kweku begged, "I need water urgently. I will pay anything you ask." It was so humiliating to have to beg to buy water and he felt mortified. But better to damage his dignity here than face Agyapomaa empty handed.

"Sorry sah," the driver shook his head resolutely. "As for my load, it has been paid for already. The man is my good customer too, so I can't disappoint him. Let me ask my friends." He hopped out of the cab and landed on the ground with a sound like a ton of cement. He was much bigger and heavier than Kweku, and ambled ponderously towards his colleagues.

The others, seeing him approach, huddled around. But he was shaking his head when he returned a few minutes later. "Massa, they are all booked. Unless Monday."

"What!" Kweku exclaimed, and just then felt his stomach rumble. There had been no opportunity to do a big job in the loo since the previous night and it appeared nature was catching up with him. "But you, don't you work on Sundays too? This is business. I know you charge more for Sunday work and I am prepared to pay. If it is too late today you can make it tomorrow."

A sneer appeared on the driver's face. "Hoh! You paa! You don't want me to go to chapel because you don't have water? As for me, I don't play with my worship oh. Sorry, but you have to find someone else."

"Please help me. I'm hot." Kweku begged, hating the grovelling he heard in his voice.

One of the chaps who had sauntered over intervened. "You can try coming here early tomorrow morning. Some of our people work on Sundays."

"Really?"

"Please," the chap said hastily, "I am not assuring you of anything, just giving you the best advice under the circumstances."

The phone vibrated in his pocket. The caller ID showed Agyapomaa. What could he tell her right then? He ignored the call. A minute later a text message came through 'Kweku I'm waitn 4 de wata'.

As he threaded his way home slowly, trying not to get there, Kweku dialled Danso's number once again. Thankfully it went through. Danso answered on the eighth ring and straight-away launched into an explanation.

"Oh Massa Kweku, sorry oh... My Massa, I mean my car owner, called me and asked me to bring him water. I couldn't say I wouldn't bring it, so I had to go and give him the water I had fetched for you."

Kweku trembled with anger. "Danso, couldn't you have gotten any of your colleagues to supply me the water? You have kept me waiting the whole day when you could easily have asked someone else to do it, to help you out."

"Massa Kweku, my Massa called me ri...ght now. I was on my way to your place when he called me."

"Danso, forget about your master. Just call one of your friends to come and supply me. I have no water at all at home."

"But Massa Kweku, this one na small problem. Tomorrow will come ri...ght now and I'll supply you the water."

"Danso, I'm talking about today and you're talking about tomorrow."

"No problem Massa Kweku. As for tomorrow coming, all you have to do is sleep. By the time you wake up it will be tomorrow and I'll bring the water." Danso hung up unceremoniously.

Just then a new text message alert beeped on his phone. 'I'm dying to take a bath. Please push Danso to hurry'.

"Harrumph!" Kweku exclaimed in impotent frustration. Hot, sticky, stinky, sweaty, itchy, and downright... there was no name for it, he felt like punching someone with all his strength.

Though born in Tamale, the capital of Ghana's Northern Region, Isaac Neequaye spent the greater part of his formative years in Kumasi, where his father taught at the Kwame Nkrumah University of Science and Technology. Secondary education took him to Accra and then back to Kumasi again, where he graduated from the electrical engineering programme at KNUST in 1991.